cathy cassidy

Sundae Girl

PUFFIN

PUFFIN BOOKS

Published by the Penguin Group
Penguin Books Ltd, 80 Strand, London WC2R ORL, England
Penguin Group (USA) Inc., 375 Hudson Street, New York, New York 10014, USA
Penguin Group (Canada), 90 Eglinton Avenue East, Suite 700, Toronto, Ontario, Canada M4P 2Y3
(a division of Pearson Penguin Canada Inc.)
Penguin Ireland, 25 St Stephen's Green, Dublin 2, Ireland (a division of Penguin Books Ltd)
Penguin Group (Australia), 250 Camberwell Road, Camberwell, Victoria 3124, Australia
(a division of Pearson Australia Group Pty Ltd)
Penguin Books India Pvt Ltd, 11 Community Centre, Panchsheel Park, New Delhi – 110 017, India
Penguin Group (NZ), 67 Apollo Drive, Rosedale, North Shore 0632, New Zealand
(a division of Pearson New Zealand Ltd)
Penguin Books (South Africa) (Pty) Ltd, 24 Sturdee Avenue, Rosebank, Johannesburg 2196, South Africa

Penguin Books Ltd, Registered Offices: 80 Strand, London WC2R ORL, England

puffinbooks.com

First published 2007
This edition produced for The Book People Ltd, Hall Wood Avenue,
Haydock, St Helens WA11 9UL

1

Text copyright © Cathy Cassidy, 2007
Illustrations copyright © Cathy Cassidy, 2007
All rights reserved

The moral right of the author/illustrator has been asserted

Set in Baskerville MT
Typeset by Palimpsest Book Production Limited,
Grangemouth, Stirlingshire
Made and printed in England by Clays Ltd, St Ives plc

British Library Cataloguing in Publication Data
A CIP catalogue record for this book is available from the British Library

ISBN: 978-1-856-13243-5

www.greenpenguin.co.uk

Penguin Books is committed to a sustainable future
for our business, our readers and our planet.
The book in your hands is made from paper
certified by the Forest Stewardship Council.

Hiya!

Do you have an embarrassing family? When I was thirteen, I thought I had the MOST embarrassing family in the world (sorry, Mum & Dad!). Guess what? These days, my kids think that *they* do . . . not fair!!!

Jude in *Sundae Girl* really does have a weird family - her grandparents are nuts, her dad thinks he's Elvis and her mum is seriously off the rails. Of course, families are never perfect and once Jude works that out, she realizes that love is what really counts . . .

Sundae Girl is based in Coventry, the city where I grew up, so it was fun to weave little threads of real-life memories in with the story. I really did go carol singing in the snow, watch *The Wizard of Oz* every Christmas and have a cool 'n' snooty Afghan hound who came from a dogs' home. Sadly there were no cute, clumsy, straw-haired admirers trailing after me on Rollerblades, but I guess you can't have everything!

I think you'll like Jude and Carter and the other crazy characters in *Sundae Girl* . . . curl up and let yourself melt into the story. Maybe life is never perfect, but y'know what? Love can get you through. (Ice cream helps as well!)

Best wishes,
Cathy Cassidy

xxxx ✿

cathycassidy.com

Thanks . . .

To Liam for endless support, hugs and for managing to drive a VW camper van around the M25 with me screaming quietly in the background. To Calum and Caitlin for surviving so well when I'm busy writing/daydreaming – you were the best first readers ever! Also, to Mum, Dad, Andy, Lori, Joan and all my fab family. You weren't really embarrassing, honest – not compared to Jude's lot! I'm lucky enough to have the best friends ever – special thanks to Helen, Sheena, Fiona, Mary-Jane, Zarah, Catriona and everyone else who has made time for fun, swims, slushy movies and heart-to-hearts over the last year. It means a whole lot to me.

Thanks to Paul for the webby work and Martyn for the maths. Thanks to Darley, 'special agent', and his sassy sidekicks Julia, Lucie, Zoe and all at the agency. Also to Rebecca, my fab editor, Adele, for the ideas, the van and the pep talks . . . and Francesca, Kirsten, Tania, Jodie, Sarah, Alison, Emily, Katya, Sara, Jennie & the whole Puffin crew! I couldn't do any of this without you.

Most of all, thanks to the kids from all around the world who email my website, write to me or come to book festivals and signings . . . your support, enthusiasm and loyalty makes all the hard work worthwhile.

Nobody likes Parents' Night, do they? It's when the truth comes out. Your parents discover that you haven't been wearing your nice maroon St Joseph's blazer, you've only handed in one maths homework since September and you're hanging out with a gang of scary Year Tens who have LOVE and HATE scrawled across their knuckles in black marker pen.

That's the kind of stuff most kids are stressing about, anyhow. Not me. I have a pretty good record when it comes to tests, homework and school uniform. My friends are sensible, reliable, hard-working. My teachers like me.

What do I have to be worried about?

Where do you want me to start?

I'm not worried that my family will find out the truth about school – I'm more anxious that school will find out the truth about my family.

Parents' Night? I hate it so much that when I was in Year Seven I threw away the letters inviting my family along and told them that St Joseph's didn't do them.

'Are you sure?' Mum had asked, doubtfully. 'That seems very strange.'

'Seriously. They think it's old-fashioned.'

Mum had raised an eyebrow, but I got away with it. I thought I might get away with it right through secondary school.

Of course, I was wrong.

Yesterday, my form teacher, Miss Devlin, booked herself into the hairdressing salon where Mum works, for a shampoo and set. 'Special occasion?' Mum had enquired, rolling a sliver of Miss Devlin's mouse-brown hair on to a pink plastic curler. 'Going somewhere nice?'

'Well,' Miss Devlin had replied, 'just the Year Eight Parents' Night at St Joseph's tomorrow.'

That was that. My cover was blown, big style.

'Why didn't you tell us they'd reintroduced Parents' Night?' Mum wanted to know. 'Just think, we might have missed it!'

Mmm. Just think.

'Poor Miss Devlin would have thought we didn't care!' Mum exclaimed. 'Don't you worry, Jude, we'll be there!'

And they are here – all of them. Nightmare.

I'm here too, watching the whole thing, fascinated, horrified. Being here is a kind of torture, obviously, but when Mr McGrath asked for volunteers to make the tea and coffee, my hand shot up instantly like the good Year Eight teacher-pleaser that I am. It's a bit like the way moths get drawn to a flame. I can't help myself, even though I know it will end in disaster and frazzled wings.

Still, dishing out the tea is one way to keep an eye on things.

I take a deep breath, steady my tea tray and stride off into the scrum, handing out a few cups of milky tea and some dark, ominous flapjacks baked earlier today in the Home Ec. department. I glide to a halt beside Miss Devlin's desk.

'Tea?' I ask brightly.

Miss Devlin shoots me a helpless, wild-eyed look, but I have no sympathy. So far, she's only met Mum. Worse is to come.

'Ah, Jude,' Mum says, flicking her blonde razor-cut bob so we all get to see the dark red layer beneath. 'Miss Devlin was just telling me that she runs the school drama club. Why ever didn't you tell her I was in show business?'

'You're a hairdresser, Mum,' I mumble.

'*Now* I am,' Mum says, exasperated. 'But what about my musical past? I've played all the top venues – Filey, Minehead, Clacton-on-Sea.'

She is talking about the weekly talent shows at

various Butlins holiday camps where she holidayed as a teenager, but she leaves out that little detail.

'Mum,' I hiss, dumping a cup of tea and a crumbling flapjack down on the tabletop. 'I thought I'd better tell you that Dad and Victoria are here. They're in the queue behind you.'

'They are?' Mum squeaks. 'Oh! Nice chatting to you, Miss Devlin. I have to go now.'

Mum and Dad are no longer together – they haven't been for twelve years, but that doesn't stop Mum from turning all drama queen if she happens to spot Dad with his girlfriend.

Mum leans across the desk, dazzling Miss Devlin with her showbiz smile. 'If you ever need some *professional* input with the drama club, I'd be only too pleased to offer my expertise!'

Miss Devlin shuffles some papers. 'Well... thanks, Ms Reilly,' she says, weakly. 'I'll be sure to let you know if we need any ... um, *professional* input.'

Mum stands up, flinging a pink pashmina scarf over her shoulder and almost taking out the eye of the woman behind. She stalks out of the hall without a backward glance.

I swing back through the crowd, clutching my tea tray. I come across Gran and Grandad arguing with Mr McGrath. I'm not sure why. He's not even one of my teachers.

'Hello, dear,' Gran says blankly as I edge past.

'D'you know, you look just like my granddaughter!'

Perhaps because I am? I give her the last flapjack and hope it doesn't get stuck in her teeth.

Back at the tea-urn, Kevin Carter from my English class is sipping tea from a PTA bone-china cup. He dunks a flapjack, unsuccessfully. The tea turns into beige soup, or perhaps some kind of wholemeal porridge.

'Hey, Jude,' he says. 'Want a hand?'

'No thanks, Carter. Keep it to yourself,' I retort.

'Call me Kevin if you like,' he grins.

'OK. Thanks, Carter.'

'Suit yourself. I'd be a good waiter, y'know. Careful. Fast.' He sticks out a leg and shows me a huge, clunky Rollerblade boot, then does a fancy turn, slopping tea all over his jeans.

'I'm just learning,' he says. 'Brendan Coyle is setting up a street hockey team.' He points through the window, where some Year Eight lads are skating about in the floodlit playground, battering each other with hockey sticks.

'Nice,' I say.

'Are your parents here?' Kevin Carter asks, pouring himself another cup of tea.

'I think they're around somewhere,' I say vaguely.

'Will you look at that!' he guffaws, looking out across the hall. 'Who does he think he is, Elvis Presley?'

Dad and Victoria have reached the head of the line for Miss Devlin. Victoria looks neat in a dark city suit, but Dad is wearing a grey raincoat over his white rhinestone catsuit. He has a gig later, an eightieth birthday party at some old folks' home. He smooths his black quiff and sideburns as he sits down.

I should explain – Dad is an Elvis impersonator. This is not a fact I tell many people. I have no intention of telling Kevin Carter, obviously.

Miss Devlin glances up, does a double take and gives Dad a forbidding look over the rim of her teacup.

'Think he's someone's dad, or just the floorshow?' Kevin Carter muses.

'No idea.' I let my hair swing forward to camouflage the blushes as I prepare a new tray, piled high with flapjacks and dishwater tea, and Carter lets out a low whistle as Year Eight siren Kristina Kowalski wiggles past. She is wearing something that might have once belonged to a Barbie Doll, but has now shrunk in the wash. Scary.

'Kristina Kowalski is *hot*!' Carter breathes, executing a perfect figure of eight on his Rollerblades before crashing into the tea-urn. Hot is not a word I'd use to describe Kristina. She is wearing so little, she may be in danger of frostbite.

Just as I think Kevin Carter is safely distracted

from my family, Gran and Grandad join the end of Miss Devlin's queue. Grandad is wearing his yellow tartan waistcoat with the Marilyn Monroe tie, and Gran is knitting as she waits. It's the green scarf, today. At only three metres long, it is easily the most portable.

'Who are *they*?' Carter gawps, following my gaze. 'Unreal! I wonder what poor kid has to put up with grandparents like that?'

My heart plummets. Carter is going to guess the exact identity of that poor kid, unless I take evasive action – and fast.

'Actually,' I tell him, 'they're Kristina Kowalski's mum and dad.'

Carter just about chokes on his tea. 'Parents?' he yelps. 'They can't be. They're way too old.'

Kristina only joined the school this term, and so far she's a bit of a mystery girl – if a girl who wears shrunken skirts and lashings of shimmering lipgloss can actually qualify as mysterious.

'Oh, yes,' I lie. 'Very strict too. Mr Kowalski used to be a championship boxer. Last month, Kristina's dad came home and found her smooching with Martin Peploe from Year Nine, when she should have been babysitting her seven little sisters. Mr Kowalski threw Martin Peploe out of the house. He landed in a rose bush – terrible scratches, and greenfly.'

7

'Seriously?' Carter marvels. 'I never heard that!'

'Would you broadcast it, if you were Kristina?' I ask. 'Or Martin Peploe, for that matter?'

'S'pose not. Maybe they grounded her, and that's why she's kind of a recluse? Seven little sisters. Wow!'

Mr McGrath looms up, and I try to look busy, setting out clean cups and saucers on a new tray.

'Ah, Carter, good to see you helping out at this kind of function.' Mr McGrath beams. 'Not like those young thugs out there with the hockey sticks. Now, Mrs Yates was just saying she'd love a nice, hot cup of tea – perhaps you'd take one over to her?'

He lifts the loaded tray and hands it to Carter, nodding encouragement. Needless to say, he hasn't spotted the Rollerblades.

Carter takes the tray, throwing me an anxious grin. He glides off across the polished floor, the tea tray balanced on one hand. He makes amazingly good progress, to start with at least, but disaster is inevitable. Suddenly, he gets tangled up with the end of Gran's green scarf and falls headlong into the crowd, showering everyone with tea and flapjacks.

'Oh dear,' says Mr McGrath.

He's not as bad as I thought, that Kevin Carter.

Don't get me wrong, I love my family. I live with Gran, Grandad, Mum and Toto in a semi-detached house in a street called Pine Tree Avenue. There are no pine trees anywhere around, except now, in December, when they are in every window, decorated with fairy lights and tinsel.

At this time of year, Grandad likes to give his name and address as Patrick Reilly, 211 Christmas Tree Avenue. This causes problems with banks, taxi drivers, delivery firms and postmen. The fact that he has a full white beard and a figure like Santa Claus does not help matters.

Gran used to be a calming influence on him, but for a few years now she's had Alzheimer's disease – Old-Timer's Disease, Grandad calls it. She's not in any kind of pain, but she forgets stuff, like names and dates and even how to get dressed properly. Not long ago, she went missing and we tracked her down in Tesco, still in her dressing gown, loading a trolley with kiwi fruit and telling an anxious shelf-stacker how to knit an Aran jumper.

I remember when Gran was the one who held the house together, the one who baked fresh scones if I brought a friend over from school, jam tarts on a Sunday. She used to make me beautiful jumpers with stripes or Fair Isle patterns, and hats and mittens and scarves and shawls for friends and relatives and neighbours. Now, it's just the scarves, and nobody really wants them. They are metres long and full of lumps and holes.

It should be Mum looking after Gran and Grandad, looking after me, but she just isn't that kind of person. She is forty-four years old, going on fourteen. Sometimes she's gorgeous and glamorous and funny. Sometimes she really is not.

In the evenings, she sits at the piano hammering out grim old Irish songs that make you want to cry into your cocoa, telling anyone who'll listen about her glory days as a singer. 'I could have been a star,' she likes to tell me. 'I won the weekly talent contest at Butlins in Clacton-on-Sea in 1981, and I often played the piano at the Irish centre. Very popular, I was. Then I met your dad, Jude, and that was the end of that.'

Now Mum works part-time in the hairdresser's on the corner, a salon called Chop Suey after its owner, Sue. Often, people ring up to order egg-fried rice and chicken noodles, and get annoyed when offered blonde highlights instead.

And Toto? He's our dog, a tall, languid Afghan hound with flowing strawberry-blonde hair. He is very beautiful, but very stupid. The dogs' home told us he was a pedigree, but that he'd run away from home so often his owner despaired of him. This appealed to Grandad, who likes a challenge.

Toto has never run away from us, perhaps because Mum brushes his hair and scooshes him with leave-in conditioner every day, or perhaps because Grandad buys him gory old bones from the butcher and walks him for miles every morning and night.

'Well,' Grandad announces, the morning after Parents' Night. 'Your teachers were full of praise, Jude. Well done.'

'Yes, well done,' Mum agrees, sipping her black coffee while the rest of us pick at our cornflakes. 'You take after me. I was always good at school too, you know.'

'Fiddlesticks!' says Gran, and Mum shoots her an angry look.

'What?' she asks, blinking sweetly, smoothing the tea-stained green scarf out across the table and brushing off the remnants of last night's flapjack crumbs. 'I dropped a stitch, that's all.'

Mum frowns and goes back to her coffee.

'I don't know what your father thinks he was doing there,' she says darkly. 'Dressed in that – that *catsuit* thing too. Whatever must your teachers have thought?'

'He had an OAP party to go to,' I say lightly. 'He was going straight on there after the school.'

'Why does he have to embarrass us like that?' Mum sulks.

'I thought you liked all that showbiz stuff,' Grandad reminds her. 'And you were just as bad yourself in the beginning, admit it! White PVC knee-boots, black minidress, blonde beehive hair . . .'

When Mum and Dad first met, Dad was in a Beatles tribute band called the Fab Four. He was supposed to be Paul McCartney – I've seen the pictures. Mum got into that whole dressing-up thing, and the band let her fill in as backing singer sometimes. Sadly, she wasn't very good, so any dreams of a career pretending to be a young Lulu or Cilla Black bit the dust pretty quickly.

'I grew out of it,' Mum says sharply. '*He* just got fat and had to give up the Fab Four to become an Elvis lookalike. How sad is that?'

'He makes a living,' I point out, thinking of the weekly cheque he sends Mum to help pay for my shoes, my winter coat, my piano lessons.

'Well, anyway, he shouldn't lurk about at Jude's Parents' Night. What did he think he was *doing*?'

'The same as us,' Grandad sighs. 'I asked him to come. He has a right, Rose – she's his daughter too.'

Mum scowls. 'I wish she wasn't.'

'You can't change it, love,' Grandad says. 'It's done. Blood is thicker than water.'

I've heard it all a million times before, but I still don't get it. Mum left Dad, all those years ago. She cancelled the wedding and scooped me into a rickety pram with a suitcase balanced on top, and she marched back home to Gran and Grandad's. It was her decision to leave – so why is she still angry, twelve years on? Beats me.

I finish my cornflakes, rifle through the stuff on the clothes airer for my gym kit.

Mum is brushing out Gran's long grey hair. Before she got ill, Gran had the most fantastic hair – she'd wear it up, in a French pleat or a wispy bun, or knotted loosely with a bright silk scarf tied round it. Now, she forgets to even brush it, so Mum does it, smoothing it, plaiting it, pinning the braids up across her head so she looks like the picture on the cover of a book I once read. Heidi, but with wrinkles.

'Ah, Molly,' Grandad sighs. 'My sweet Irish colleen.'

'Who's Molly?' Gran asks brightly. 'Do I know her?'

'You're Molly, pet,' Grandad says sadly. He stacks up the breakfast plates and dumps them into the sink.

'All I'm saying,' Mum huffs, 'is that if he insists on turning up at Jude's school, he should at least leave *that woman* behind.'

'Victoria is a lovely girl,' Grandad says firmly. Victoria is a bank clerk in Grandad's local branch. 'Very kind. And she's always been good to our Jude, hasn't she?'

Victoria is great, but Mum definitely doesn't want to hear that. Not this morning, and not from me. Unless I can tell her that Victoria eats raw liver for supper and tortures small animals as a hobby, my comments are not wanted here. I stay silent.

'That dreadful suit she was wearing,' Mum says. 'And her hair! Why can't she get it done professionally?'

'She looked very nice to me,' Grandad says.

'And that engagement ring was just *beautiful*,' Gran chips in.

Mum drops the hairbrush, and it clatters on to the floor. We all stare at Gran, eyes wide with horror, but she's gazing down at her knitting again, brows furrowed. She might as well be a million miles away.

Mum makes a kind of choking sound. 'Engagement ring?' she gasps. 'I didn't see an engagement ring. Did you?'

We shake our heads, stunned into silence.

'He wouldn't. Would he, Jude?'

'No,' I whisper, but I don't know, not really. Dad loves Victoria, I know that. She loves him. Why shouldn't they get married? But . . . wouldn't he tell me first?

'Take no notice of your gran,' Mum says boldly. 'She's always getting things mixed up. The very idea!'

I pick up my bag from the coat peg in the hall. Mum's right – Gran does get muddled up. Not this time, though. Something tells me that this time Gran's not muddled up at all.

Everyone is talking about the Green Scarf Incident from yesterday's Parents' Night. Kevin Carter's fateful fall has been transformed from something clumsy and embarrassing into something wonderful, heroic. Carter has a bandaged right arm and gets out of work for hours, until someone remembers he's left-handed.

By late afternoon, the true identity of the batty old couple with the green scarf at the centre of the action is at last revealed. Kristina Kowalski, glancing down at me like I'm something disgusting she just scraped off her spike-heeled shoe, is not impressed.

'You told Carter they were my *parents*,' she hisses. 'You sad little loser.'

'I . . . er . . . thought he was talking about someone else,' I bluff.

'Yeah, right,' Kristina says. 'And I do not have seven little sisters, OK? I'm an only child. Really, Jude, I pity you.'

She wiggles on up to the back of the English room and perches on Brendan Coyle's desk. Her skirt, another shrunk-in-the-wash special, slides up scarily to reveal acres of fake-tan thigh. Kristina Kowalski is the only girl I know who comes to school in December wearing high heels, ankle socks and a micro-mini. I hope she gets icicles on her bum.

'Ignore her,' Nuala O'Sullivan says, beside me. 'Everyone has grandparents. What's the big deal?'

'No big deal,' I sigh.

'And anyway, that thing with the scarf was a useful diversion.' Nuala grins. 'It took the heat off your dad. If Kristina ever finds out about him . . .'

'Don't. It doesn't bear thinking about.'

'Oh, Jude, you worry too much,' she laughs. She can afford to – she has a normal mum and dad with normal jobs and normal dress sense.

Miss Devlin sweeps into the classroom, a small, fierce whirlwind dressed entirely in navy blue. 'Miss Kowalski, back to your own seat,' she snaps. 'And Miss Kowalski – I wonder if you could remember to wear a skirt tomorrow? Knee-length, grey, regulation. If you forget yet again, perhaps I could find something in the lost-property cupboard for you?'

'No thanks, *Miss* Devlin,' Kristina replies. 'I'll remember.' She makes it sound like a threat.

We settle down to write an essay called 'School Uniform: For or Against?' I surprise myself by coming out in favour of knee-length grey skirts, stripy ties and hideous maroon blazers. In uniform, you can blend in, become invisible. You look just like everyone else . . . even if you're really not.

'I hate uniform,' Nuala whispers. 'Who wants to be a sheep?'

I do. I really, really do.

At the end of the lesson, we hand in our books and put our chairs up on the desks, because it's the end of the day. The bell rings out, but we never get away that lightly, not with Miss Devlin. St Joseph's is a Catholic school, and Miss Devlin is an old-style Catholic. She makes us join our hands, close our eyes and pray silently.

When the shuffling and coughing dies down, I pray for Gran and Grandad, Mum and Dad and Victoria and Toto. I pray that Gran was wrong, even though I'm not sure what's so scary about the idea of Dad getting married. It just is.

'Let us finish,' Miss Devlin says, 'by offering up a special prayer for Kevin Carter, so that his wrist heals quickly. For Brendan Coyle, so that he learns to stop wasting time in my lesson. And Kristina Kowalski, so that she finds her school skirt and her manners. We pray to St Jude – the patron saint of hopeless cases. Amen.'

There's a snort of laughter from Brendan Coyle and then we're dismissed, clattering down the stairs and out towards the school gates.

I'm halfway down the street when Kevin Carter skates up and gives me a high five with his bandaged hand.

'That prayer worked quickly,' I observe.

'Aw, it was just a scam. Thought I'd go for the sympathy vote. So, how come your parents named you after the patron saint of hopeless cases? That's a bit mean.'

'They didn't,' I say shortly. I've heard it all before, this stuff about St Jude, and I refuse to be bugged by it.

'So how come . . .'

'Dad named me after his favourite song,' I explain. 'It was a Beatles track called "Hey Jude". Mum didn't mind because her favourite film star was called Judy Garland. There were no saints involved, OK?'

'OK.' Kevin Carter nods, but seems in no hurry to move off. I walk on, and he skates along beside me, tripping occasionally on uneven paving stones.

'I wanted to say sorry,' he admits at last. 'About last night, y'know?'

'It's not your fault you're useless on Rollerblades.'

'Not about the fall,' he says. 'I mean, I am sorry about that, but . . . it was the laughing at your grandparents, really. I didn't realize.'

I raise one eyebrow. 'Doesn't matter,' I say. 'They are odd. That's just the way it is. Could have been worse.'

He could have clocked that Elvis was my dad.

'Was he really a championship boxer? Your grandad?'

Grandad worked for the post his whole life, but Kevin Carter's not to know that.

'Might have been.'

'OK. Well, I know you don't have seven little sisters – you're an only child, like Kristina. But the rest of the story . . . the bit about watching *Neighbours* with Martin Peploe from Year Nine. Was that you?'

I stare at Kevin Carter, amazed. He thinks I once sat on a sofa with Martin Peploe? I can feel myself going pink. It's the best compliment anyone ever gave me.

'You don't have to talk about it if you don't want.' Carter shrugs. 'Some things are private.'

'They are,' I agree.

'But I'd like you to know that I think Martin Peploe has excellent taste.'

Carter winks, scarily, and skates off down the road like someone just put a rocket down his trousers. He gets right down to the junction before colliding with a pillar box.

'I'm getting better,' he shouts over as I cross the street.

Better than what? I wonder, but I know what St Jude would say. Better than hopeless.

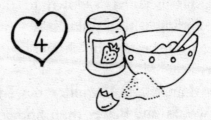

Dad lives in a little terraced house near the city centre. When I ring the doorbell, the chime plays 'Blue Suede Shoes'.

'Jude, sweetheart!' Dad says, opening the door in jeans and a T-shirt that says *Elvis Lives*. 'Come in, my little child-genius. Your teachers were pleased with you last night. Me and Vic were so proud!'

'Don't be daft,' I laugh. 'Thanks for coming, anyway.'

Now that it's over, I guess I *am* glad Dad and Victoria were there. I just wish they'd blended into the background a bit more.

'Didn't mind the white flares, did you?' Dad asks, reading my mind. 'I don't think anyone noticed.'

'Of course not.' White nylon catsuits with rhinestone-studded stand-up collars are all the rage among the parents at St Joseph's. 'How was the gig at the old folks' home?'

'Not bad,' Dad shrugs. 'They soon warmed up. Had them jiving round their Zimmer frames in the end, you know how it is.'

I do. I used to love going along to gigs with Dad. He is a very good Elvis impersonator, I'll give him that. He has the craziest clothes, the widest flares, the biggest quiff. He wiggles his hips and old ladies (and some young ones) squeal and roar with laughter. He works the crowd, crooning 'Love Me Tender' and gazing into the eyes of some old battleaxe, and next thing you know she's giggling like a teenager and blushing to the roots of her purple rinse.

Dad loves it, all this Elvis stuff, and his enthusiasm is catching. Except to me. These days, I am immune.

We drift through to the kitchen.

'Toast?' asks Dad, loading up the toaster and setting out the jam and butter.

'OK.'

We sit and eat toast that's dripping with butter and slathered with strawberry jam. It is a secret vice we have, the two of us. Dad reckons I must have inherited it from him, along with the black hair and freckles.

'So,' he says, crunching happily. 'How's school?'

'Great,' I lie brightly. 'How's work?'

'Busy. Always is, in the run-up to Christmas. I'm booked out – office parties, old folks' homes, discos, karaoke, the lot. Still, it should be fun!'

'Should be,' I echo.

'Jude, love,' Dad says. 'Is something bothering you?'

'No. At least . . . can I ask you a question?'

'Sure! Fire away.' Dad grins.

'Why did Mum leave you?'

I'm not sure where that came from, because actually I'm here to ask if he's getting married to Victoria. Digging up the dim and distant past is not part of the plan. Dad stares down at his toast crumbs, shell-shocked.

'Things didn't work out,' he tells me, which is all that anyone has ever been able to tell me. Suddenly, it just isn't enough.

'Why didn't they?' I push. 'Did you stop loving her? Did you have an affair?'

'No!' Dad sounds angry. 'Nothing like that, Jude. Perhaps you should ask your mum.'

'I'm asking you,' I remind him.

'Yes, you are.'

'So?'

'So . . . oh, Jude, we cared a lot about each other. We met after a Fab Four gig. We were together for years, having fun, out every night, touring with the band. Then you came along, and everything should have been perfect. We were planning to get married – a church wedding, a white dress for Rose, the lot.'

I want to remind him that weddings are meant to come before babies, but I bite my tongue. Instead I try to picture myself as the littlest bridesmaid ever, pink-faced and beaming in a dress full of frills.

'What went wrong?'

Dad sighs. 'Looking after a baby isn't easy. Your mum was a bit wiped out at first, she found it hard to cope. I was away a lot, with the band, so I couldn't help as much as I'd have liked. She started drinking. I mean, we'd always liked a drink, the two of us, so I didn't notice it to start with, but then I realized Rose was drinking in the day.

'You can't do that when you've got a baby to look after, Jude. I got scared. I started taking more and more time off from the band, to look after you, until finally they found someone else to take my place.'

Dad lets his shoulders sag, remembering.

'Go on,' I say quietly. I want to hear it all, now we've got started. It's my history, after all.

'We put the wedding off, till things got better,' Dad remembers. 'Only – well, they never did. I couldn't stand it, the way she was drinking, kidding herself that everything was fine. One day, we argued over breakfast. I poured all the drink in the house away, and Rose packed a suitcase and took you home to her parents.'

Mum left Dad because he wouldn't let her have whisky for breakfast. It's not what I imagined, but then again, it's not exactly a shock. Mum doesn't drink these days, but that's because the doctor says she can't. She's messed up her body with years and years of it, of drinking and weeping softly into the bottom of a whisky glass.

I always thought she drank because of Dad. Now I know it's because of *me*.

'Jude?' Dad is looking at me intently. 'You said you wanted to know. I'm sorry.'

'Me too.'

'I didn't want to let you go,' Dad says. 'It broke my heart, but I knew Molly and Patrick would look after you – and Rose, of course. It seemed like the best thing at the time.' He reaches out across the table and squeezes my hand.

'I always thought it was something *you* did,' I say shakily.

'So did I, Jude. So did I.'

When Victoria gets in from work, she finds us baking sponge cake from a dog-eared recipe book. Things have not gone well. I do not have

Gran's gift for baking, and Dad doesn't have the right kind of flour, the right amount of eggs, the right kind of sandwich tins. And we've eaten all the strawberry jam. We press on regardless, pouring the mixture into a non-stick loaf-tin, whipping up butter and icing sugar and cocoa powder to make buttercream icing to die for.

'Hi, Jude.' Victoria grins, chucking her jacket on the sofa and kicking off her shoes. 'Smells gorgeous. What's the occasion?'

'Oh, nothing much,' I say airily. 'We're just celebrating something.'

Victoria shoots a quizzical look at Dad, who pretends not to notice. 'So, what are we celebrating?' she asks again.

'Nothing important,' I tease. 'Just the fact that you're finally going to make an honest man of my dad!'

'You told her!' Victoria squeals. 'Oh, Jude, what do you think? Are you OK with it? Because if you think it's too soon . . .'

'Soon? You've been living together for six years!'

'I know, but if you'd rather we waited . . .'

'Victoria! I'm trying to tell you how happy I am. OK?'

'OK!' She flings her arms round me and hugs me tight, and I wonder how I ever could have thought this was a bad idea. Victoria and Dad are perfect for each other.

'Want to see the ring?' She blushes, showing me her left hand with the tiny diamond glinting. 'Isn't it beautiful?'

'Gorgeous,' I tell her.

'You're gorgeous,' Dad corrects me, putting an arm round each of us. 'My two gorgeous girls.'

Just then, the oven timer goes off and I dive for an oven glove to rescue the cake. I lift it out, golden brown, looking like a small, steaming housebrick with a worrying dent in the middle.

'It'll be fine once we've got the icing on,' Dad says doubtfully.

'Of course it will,' Victoria says kindly. 'What exactly is it, anyway?'

My mouth twitches, and Dad is unable to keep a straight face. Soon we're doubled up, laughing, and all I can do is point to the recipe book, the page splattered now with chocolate buttercream and bits of eggshell.

It's Victoria Sponge.

It is almost Christmas. I know this because I have watched the sixth-form pantomime, burned a trayful of mince pies in Home Ec. and learnt 'Silent Night' in German. I stood behind a stall at the Christmas Craft Fair, flogging handprinted gift wrap and salt-dough Santas and home-made crackers filled with pick 'n' mix.

On the last day of term, we get to finish early. Year Seven and Year Nine are having an afternoon Christmas disco in the school hall. Years Ten and Eleven are having an *evening* Christmas disco in the school hall. Year Eight are raising money for an orphanage in China, so we get to troop into the city centre with photocopied carol sheets and collecting tins, even though the temperature is sub-zero. Kristina Kowalski, after weeks of wiggling about in black hipsters, has appeared once more in her micro-mini, and may well need to be wrapped in one of those reflective blankets they drape round accident victims if she is foolish enough to venture outside.

'This is it, 8b.' Miss Devlin beams, as we trudge on to coaches hired specially to take us to our fate. 'The real spirit of Christmas.'

Year Eight is divided into three groups and dropped off at different locations around the city to divide and conquer. Two classes get to sing in the foyer at the railway station, where travellers are returning home for Christmas full of smiles and loose change. Two classes are dropped at a supermarket complex heaving with festive shoppers, and get to rattle their tins where it is warm and cosy. The last two, 8a and 8b, get to shiver in the open air in the middle of the shopping precinct in town.

Miss Devlin, wearing novelty reindeer antlers on her mousy curls, darts in and out of the harassed shoppers, shaking a tin. A couple of kids play violins with frostbitten fingers, which sounds like several cats being strangled.

We trawl through 'Silent Night', 'Little Donkey' and 'Away in a Manger', then throw in 'White Christmas' for light relief. After an hour, flasks of hot cocoa and weighty fruit cake are passed around to keep us going. Kristina Kowalski pretends to have a sore throat and is sent home early, her legs mottled blue like slabs of Stilton cheese.

The rest of us struggle on, even when the light begins to fade and the first flakes of snow begin to fall.

'Keep going,' Miss Devlin implores. 'Just half an hour more. Think of those little orphans. Think of the true spirit of Christmas!'

If I hear another word about the true spirit of Christmas I think I will cry. My tears will probably turn to icicles as they fall.

Across the way, a small man in a bobble hat and striped scarf starts selling the evening paper from a makeshift stand.

'City Final!' he roars, over the sound of our singing.

'Hark the Herald!' Brendan Coyle roars back.

Eventually, even Miss Devlin admits that it's too cold to go on. The snow is falling fast now, and shoppers are hurrying for their buses and cars, anxious to get home. They don't want to hear carols, or cats being strangled.

'Happy Christmas, children,' Miss Devlin calls out, her antlers bobbing. 'Take care getting home. See you in the New Year!'

We break up into little groups and slither through the slush down towards the bus stops. Nuala O'Sullivan flags down a number 73 and I am left alone, at the tail end of the longest queue I have ever seen for the number 32A. Every bus that comes past is stuffed with shoppers. One after another sweeps past, splattering me with grey slush. I am so cold I could curl up in a corner and die.

'We could always walk,' says a voice in my ear.

Kevin Carter is at my side, a black beanie hat pulled low over straw-coloured hair, coat collar turned up against the snow.

'Sure. Nice weather for a stroll,' I snap.

'Seriously,' Carter says. 'The buses are full – you'll be stuck here till all hours. We could start walking, warm up a bit. If we stick to the bus route, we'll be able to get on eventually, once people start getting off.'

'Carter, it's *miles*,' I protest.

'You can call me Kevin,' he grins.

'I know. C'mon, Carter, it's a crazy idea.'

'Got a better one?'

I haven't. We walk down through the precinct, almost deserted now, and out along the main road towards Tile Hill. The snow is settling, hiding grey pavements beneath a shimmering crust of white.

'You don't even catch the same bus as me,' I accuse him.

'No,' he admits.

'Were you following me?'

Carter pulls a big red envelope, slightly soggy,

from his pocket. 'Wanted to give you this,' he says. 'I forgot, in school. Just a card, y'know.'

I open the card, which shows two penguins standing together on a heart-shaped chunk of ice. There is a foil-wrapped chocolate tree decoration inside the envelope, also heart-shaped.

'Thanks,' I say. 'I haven't got anything for you.'

'S'OK.' Carter shrugs. 'I didn't expect anything. What are you doing at Christmas?'

'The usual. Falling asleep in midnight Mass, eating too much turkey, watching too much corny TV. You?'

'Pretty much the same. How about New Year?'

I roll my eyes. 'Party,' I tell him. 'My dad just got engaged to his girlfriend, and they're having a get-together. Fancy dress.' It's an Elvis party, actually, but I leave out that little detail.

'Your dad?' Carter frowns.

'He's not with my mum any more,' I explain. 'Not for years.'

'That's why you live with your grandparents?'

'That's why.'

'Can anyone come?' Carter asks. 'To the party?'

'Strictly invite only.'

'Pity.'

We've turned off the main road now, heading down the hill towards my old school, Our Lady of Sorrows.

'Kristina Kowalski lives around here somewhere,' Carter says.

'Does she?' I reply. 'What a thrill! I've never seen her around.'

'Nobody knows much about her,' Carter muses. 'Even Brendan doesn't know where she lives exactly.'

'In a crumbling castle full of dungeons, bats and vampires?' I suggest.

'You don't like her, do you?'

'Well spotted!'

'She's OK.' Carter shrugs, and even though I don't like Kevin Carter, not really, I feel a sharp needle of jealousy. Kristina Kowalski can have any boy she wants – I just don't want her to have Carter.

'Wow. Our Lady of Sorrows?' Carter reads from the snowcapped sign as we trudge past the grey building-block classrooms. 'Some name for a primary school! Bet that was a bundle of laughs.'

'It was OK,' I tell him. 'We called it "Our Lady's" for short.'

'Wish I'd known you when you were six years old, with gaps in your teeth and pigtails.' Carter grins. 'What's this bit – the church?' We stop, looking up at the stained-glass windows, the fancy zigzaggy roof that some architect must have thought would look really cool back in the 1960s.

'Yeah. Mass every Sunday, class service on

Tuesdays, Benediction on Fridays,' I tell him. 'We never go any more.'

Not since the time Gran shouted out in the middle of an especially heated sermon, telling Father Lynch to mind his manners or she'd have a word with his mum.

'Me neither,' Carter says.

'It was different back then,' I tell him. 'I believed it all. I saw a miracle here once, when I was seven.'

'What kind of a miracle?'

I steer him off the road, across the car park and round to the back of the church. 'What am I looking for?' he asks, puzzled.

A little lantern is built into the wall, spilling yellow light into the darkness. There is a shrine built into the rocks against the back wall of the church, a statue of Our Lady of Sorrows in a blue dress, arms outstretched. Today, of course, she is shrouded in white.

'Wow!' Carter says. 'There's nothing like that at our local church.'

'It was out of bounds when we were at school, but we used to sneak through the fence.' Back then, I used to kneel at the handrail in front of the statue, praying that I'd get a Barbie for Christmas, that my hamster wouldn't die. Other stuff, too. It didn't work.

'So – what was the miracle?'

'When I was seven, some kids started a rumour that if you could make the statue smile, all your prayers would be answered,' I explain. 'I believed it. One Saturday, Nuala and I brought biscuits and Fanta and sat on the bench for hours, telling her jokes and funny stories, pulling faces, till we were so bored our eyes ached. Then – finally – she smiled!'

Carter grins. 'Not really,' he says.

'Well, maybe not really. Maybe we were just tired and fed up and over-imaginative. But we thought it happened, both of us.'

I guess I needed something to believe in, back then. It was at a time when Mum was drinking heavily, rowing lots with her old boyfriend Tom. I tried to believe I'd seen the statue smile, tried to believe my prayers would be answered. They weren't – well, not for long, anyhow.

Carter frowns up at the statue, considering. 'What d'you call a reindeer in a blindfold?' he asks, then provides his own answer. 'No-eye deer!'

'What are you doing?'

'Getting her to smile, of course!' Carter says. 'Think she could get me into the street hockey team?'

'Hmm. That might take more than a miracle.'

We trudge through the car park and back to

the pavement. Carter's hat is caked with snow, his coat flecked with white. He sticks his tongue out in the dark, catching snowflakes.

I scuff up a wad of snow on the toe of my boot, then flick it off into the road. 'Carter, why are you walking me home?' I ask.

'Felt like it,' he says, looking at me with shiny hazel eyes. He reaches out a soggy gloved hand to touch my face. 'You've got a snowflake on your nose.' He shows me the snowflake, clinging to the damp black wool of his glove like a tiny, fallen star.

'Amazing, isn't it?' Carter says. I glance up and notice the snowflakes glinting around the edge of his beanie hat, the little white flecks that cling to the tips of his long brown lashes.

Just for a moment, I think he's going to kiss me. He leans forward, his lips parted slightly, smiling, and my heart thumps, because I'm just not ready for this and I don't know how to tell him without hurting his feelings.

'Don't,' I say. 'Please.'

'I can't help it.'

Then he stuffs a snowball down the back of my neck, and runs away through the snowstorm. Typical.

My Christmas stocking holds a tangerine, chocolate coins, gel pens, nail varnish and tinsel-trimmed hairslides. Under the tree, there is a *Concise Encyclopaedia for Students* (Grandad), neon-pink curling tongs that look like an instrument of torture (Mum) and a polka-dot skipping rope (Gran).

We've all slept in, because we stayed up late at midnight Mass. We eat cornflakes, tangerines and selection box sweeties for breakfast, and it's past eleven before anyone remembers the turkey. Grandad lifts it out of the fridge, pale and goose-pimpled and reproachful.

'We have to make stuffing,' I say, looking for instructions on the side of the packet. 'Boiling water and a lump of butter, and mix it up with a fork.' I put the kettle on.

'You're only supposed to have turkey at Christmas,' Gran says, helpfully. 'It's such a lot of bother.'

'You can say that again, Molly, love. Rose!' Grandad calls through to Mum. 'Can you remember how long the turkey needs?'

'Hours, I think,' she says vaguely. 'If we put it in now, it should be ready for three.' She wanders through, cradling a black coffee and massaging her forehead. She didn't show up for midnight Mass – she was on a girls' night out with Sue from the hairdresser's.

'Gas mark four, do you think?' Grandad puzzles. He shovels in a few spoonfuls of stuffing and lifts the turkey into the roasting tin. It's disgusting, all white and clammy, like a vastly overweight chicken. You can see where its feet have been chopped off, and its head. Suddenly, I am thinking of turning vegetarian.

The last time we had roast chicken, it came golden brown and crispy, from the chippy on the corner. The time before, it was cold cuts from Tesco. It is a long time since we've tried to cook meat from scratch. How do people manage it?

Grandad peels some spuds and sticks them in the roasting tin around the turkey, then slams the whole thing into the oven. I tip a packet of frozen sprouts into a saucepan for later, and sit the Christmas pud on top of the microwave.

'Dad, Mum, Jude, you're missing the film!' Mum shouts.

It's not like missing the film would be a problem – we've seen it a million times already. It's Mum's favourite, *The Wizard of Oz*, and it used to be on TV every Christmas when she was a kid. Now it's still on every Christmas, and quite a few other days too, because Mum's boyfriend Giovanni (he's Italian) bought her the DVD.

The adults squash up on the sofa and I stretch out on the floor with Toto. He is named after the dog in the film, which is unsettling because the original Toto is a small, dishevelled terrier and our Toto is long-faced and mournful with flowing hair, a kind of canine supermodel.

For a while, there is no sound except the quiet clickety-click of Gran's knitting needles and Judy Garland in the film singing 'Over the Rainbow'. It's a musical, the kind of film that's magical when you're six years old and seriously hard work when you're twelve. It's about a girl called Dorothy and her dog Toto, who get whisked away from their dull black-and-white world by a hurricane, and dumped in the land of Oz where everything is rainbow bright.

'Why can't my life switch into glorious Technicolor?' Mum asks with a sigh. 'Why is everything always so . . . dull?'

Meanwhile, Dorothy puts on her ruby slippers

and sets off along a yellow-brick road to find the Emerald City and a wizard who can help her get back home. Along the way, she meets a scarecrow with straw for brains, a tin man with no heart and a lion with no courage.

'Story of my life,' Mum says, like she always does. 'Your dad was the scarecrow, Jude – shocking dress sense, and no more sense than he was born with. And Tom . . .'

Tom was a handsome waster in a leather jacket I remember vaguely from childhood. 'Tom's the tin man,' Mum declares. 'No heart. As for Giovanni – he's the lion. No backbone.'

'Giovanni is a good boy,' Grandad says. 'He has his own business!'

'An ice-cream van,' Mum says scathingly. 'I'm looking for something more. Pity all the men I meet are such no-hopers.'

We watch in silence as Dorothy finally finds her way back home, where life turns black and white once more, but Dorothy doesn't care, because it's where she wants to be.

Mum is misty-eyed. She slopes over to the piano, sits down and spreads her fingers over the keys. Then she launches into 'Over the Rainbow', singing raggedly, gazing up at the framed film poster of Judy Garland from *The Wizard of Oz* that hangs above the piano.

'How about you, Jude?' Grandad asks, hopefully. 'Want to give us some Christmas carols? One of your Grade Four exam pieces?'

But Mum is on a roll, running through 'Over the Rainbow' again and again before subsiding into endless slit-your-wrist Irish songs. Grandad shakes his head and goes to check on the turkey, but it's not ready yet, so we open a bottle of ginger beer and pour it into mugs. Alcohol is banned in our house, even at Christmas, on account of Mum's problem.

We have mince pies, warm from the microwave, and cream, sitting back to pull crackers and watch the Queen's speech. Grandad huffs and grumbles and swears under his breath all the way through. It's his favourite part of Christmas.

We play Cluedo and Pontoon and Charades, and Mum styles my hair into corkscrew ringlets with the neon-pink curling tongs and twines tinsel into Toto's hair. It's past seven by the time we're ready to eat. The turkey sits in the middle of the table, dark and dry and blistered. Around it, the roast potatoes are black and shrivelled, and the dish of sprouts looks like sludge-green soup.

'Everything done to perfection,' Grandad says proudly, but he has to saw at the turkey just to get through the leathery skin. He wrenches off a clump of meat and offers it to Mum.

'Well, I'm not all that hungry . . .' she blusters.

He transfers the meat to Gran's plate, along with some charred spuds and a puddle of congealed sprouts. Gran looks distressed. We stare down at our plates, unwilling to admit defeat. I decide this isn't the moment to discuss going veggie.

Grandad chokes down a mouthful of turkey, grinning weakly.

'Perhaps a bit overdone,' he says.

'We could buy it ready-cooked from Tesco, next year,' Mum suggests. 'Eat it cold, with salad. That'd be easy.'

Christmas never used to be like this.

When Gran was well, it was a feast of golden turkey, onion gravy, roasted spuds and perfect vegetables. One year, Gran helped me to make mashed-potato snowmen, with strips of roasted red pepper for scarves and cloves for eyes and buttons. Everybody said they were the best thing ever. We used to do our own Christmas pud too, as well as a big iced cake and special mincemeat with grated orange rind and tons of fruit and spices.

In those days, the Christmas tree was always real – it smelt of pine needles and dark forests, and we draped it in tinsel and cotton-wool snow and bright, tiny baubles from the special box in the attic. Every year I made decorations at school – salt-dough Santas and glittery stars and snowflakes snipped from folded paper. Gran used to laugh and hug me and hang them on the tree like they were the most beautiful things she'd ever seen.

This year, we've got a little tinsel tree from the supermarket. It sits in the corner, looking bright and shiny and slightly lopsided, and the handmade angel and the crumpled snowflakes and stars just look kind of sad.

The doorbell goes, and Toto starts to bark. It's Giovanni, Mum's Italian boyfriend, the one with no backbone, bringing ice cream and red roses and a huge box of Thorntons chocolates.

'I thought I'd bring supper,' he says, placing a tub of creamy-yellow Italian ice cream down on the table. 'But I see you haven't finished dinner yet?'

'We haven't even *started*,' Grandad exclaims. 'Will you join us, lad?'

He picks up the plates and carries them through to the kitchen, scraping the meat and sprouts and spuds on to Toto's dish. Then he takes a couple of tins out of the cupboard, loads up the toaster and sets out clean plates and cutlery. He flings an old tea towel over the turkey corpse, and carries it away. I hear the front door click, and the lid of the wheelie bin as Grandad disposes of the evidence.

Gran knits serenely, her Christmas hat askew, smiling at nothing like the Ghost of Christmas Past. Can she remember the days when we made mince pies together, ate turkey and stuffing and roast spuds so crispy, so perfect? I remember, but only just, and the memories are jumbled up with flashes of Mum fighting with Tom, her ex, in the street, falling asleep on the sofa in front of *The Wizard of Oz*.

The past is another story, and I'm not always sure I've got the plot straight.

At last, we sit down to Christmas dinner, with Giovanni at the head of the table. It's beans on toast, served with mugs of ginger beer and Christmas pudding and Italian ice cream for afters.

It's the best I've ever had.

Victoria is dancing around the living room of the flat in a red minidress and a towering black nylon wig that looks like something a guard should be wearing outside Buckingham Palace.

'This hairdo's called a beehive,' Victoria tells me. 'It was all the rage in the sixties. Very elegant, very cool! Your dad bought me the wig for Christmas.'

'It's probably not too late to take it back to the shop,' I say.

Victoria picks up a fluffy pink cushion from the sofa and chucks it at me. 'Cheeky!' she says.

Earlier on, she helped me put my hair up in big, scary rollers and now we are trying to do our make-up – pale faces, white lipstick and loads of black eyeliner all round our eyes so we look like cool 1960s chicks. Or pandas, maybe. Victoria is waving a mascara wand about as she dances.

Dad has already cracked open the wine, but Victoria isn't drinking. She never does – I guess that makes her the exact polar opposite of Mum.

I wonder if that's why Dad chose her? Probably.

Dad comes in with a platter of warm sausage rolls and a plate of cheese butties, which he puts down on the table with a flourish. He has a red apron tied round his best Elvis catsuit, the black one with the stand-up collar and the fringy flares. His black quiff is solid with hairspray, and his sideburns are long and thick and lush. He looks grim, but I don't care, because he's happy, and besides, there's nobody here from school to see him and laugh.

The CD switches to 'Blue Suede Shoes' and Dad twirls Victoria round the room a couple of times before wiggling off to the kitchen to fetch more party food.

I stand in front of the mirror to unwind the big rollers from my hair, then brush it through. It's very big, very sixties, very scary. I am wearing a black minidress with big white polka dots, white lacy tights and flat black boots.

'Perfect,' says Dad, shimmying past with trifle and chocolate cake.

'Hideous,' I correct him.

Victoria places a finger against my white-painted lips. 'Shhh,' she whispers. 'No grumbles. It's New Year's Eve. We're going to have fun. OK?'

'OK.'

The doorbell rings and the first crowd of

47

partygoers arrives, middle-aged neighbours and friends of Dad and Victoria, all wearing short dresses with flicky, bouffant hair like Priscilla Presley (Mrs Elvis, to you) or stick-on sideburns and chest wigs, like the man himself. Dad has left a basket of Elvis wigs and dark glasses by the door for the uninspired, but most people have made an effort. Guests keep coming – Hawaiian Elvis, GI Elvis, Fat Elvis, even Dead Elvis, complete with halo, harp and white fluffy wings.

It's not my sort of party, obviously, but I fix a cheesy smile on my face and offer round the crisps and nuts, making small talk with catsuit-clad strangers and people I meet once a year who tell me how I've grown. I'm the one who remembers the baked potatoes are still in the oven, and rescues them before they get burned to a crisp. I'm the one who grates cheese for the spuds, refills the ice-cube tray with water and runs down to the corner shop for more plastic cups when the first lot run out.

'OK there, Jude?' Victoria asks me as we pass in a squash of people in the hall. 'Want to come and dance?'

'Later,' I tell her. It's eleven o'clock, and a posse of large, beehived women have taken over the living room, dancing round their handbags in pointy stilettos. If one stood on you by mistake, it'd break every bone in your foot.

I give up on trying to be a party animal and make myself a hot chocolate and a round of toast and jam. Getting it upstairs is tough. I have to climb over white-quiffed Elvis and blue-rinsed Priscilla squashed in together on the stairs, snogging the face off each other. I have to convince people I'm definitely *not* in the queue for the loo.

My room has been invaded by mounds of coats and jackets. I lift them carefully and ditch them in Dad and Victoria's room, where Hawaiian Elvis lies snoring, spreadeagled across the duvet. Nice.

Finally, I shut the door behind me and take a deep breath. I am not a party girl. My face is aching from hours of smiling, making small talk with respectable middle-aged people dressed up in rhinestone flares. Enough is enough.

'Will you be OK?' Dad asked me earlier, before the guests started coming. 'I thought you'd ask some friends along, someone your own age. That nice Nuala girl, maybe?'

'Nuala's busy,' I lied. 'I'll be fine, Dad. Don't worry about me!'

The truth is, I don't want my friends at this party, not even Nuala. They'd think it was crazy, weird, bizarre. They'd laugh. And I'd feel like they were laughing at me.

Better to do it alone.

I want to be here, for Dad, for Victoria. I want

to see their friends and smile and laugh and offer round the cheese straws. I'll definitely go downstairs again before midnight, because I love the bit where everyone sings 'Auld Lang Syne' and I want to be the first to hug Dad and Victoria and wish them a Happy New Year. Until midnight, though, I'm hiding out, eating toast and sipping hot chocolate in a tiny box room in the dark.

It's the last day of the old year, the eve of the new one. There's a sheet of blue notepaper on the bed, my New Year's Resolutions. Although it's dark in here, I can see what I've written in the light from the lamp post outside.

1. Be the best-ever bridesmaid for Dad and Victoria (if they ask me).
2. Give Gran more hugs.
3. Use the curling tongs Mum gave me at least once a week so she thinks I like them. Hide her *Wizard of Oz* DVD.
4. Learn to cook so there are no more turkey disasters.
5. Pass my Grade Four piano exam (with Merit).

The problem with writing resolutions is that it's hard to know where to stop. There are so many things I'd like to change about my life it would be a full-time job fixing them all. Actually, it's other people's lives I'd like to change, and that's even harder. One thing I've learned about other people is that they rarely do what you want them to. They have ideas of their own.

There is a loud crash from the street outside, and I go to the window to look down at the frosty street. A crowd of wheelie bins have fallen over, and a couple of wisps of balled-up Christmas wrap are blowing around the pavement. A lanky figure in a black beanie hat grapples with one of the bins, struggling to haul it back up again.

My heart is thumping. This boy is haunting me. What is he doing in the street outside my dad's house at 11.30 on New Year's Eve? If I could control other people, I'd make Kevin Carter back off and leave me alone. Or get him to give up Rollerblading before he breaks his neck. Or both.

I hide behind the curtain, although it's dark in here and there's no way he could see me if he looked up. I am safe. He looks up, and I jump back from the window like I've been stung.

It's not that Kevin Carter is awful. He is not a geek, he is not a loser. He's almost good looking, in a lazy, floppy, blonde kind of way. It's just that I'm not ready for this, for long-legged boys skating around on the pavement outside my dad's house, upsetting the bins, the neighbours and the whole balance of life as I know it.

I don't want it. Do I?

If he comes inside, he'll meet my dad and any last hopes that I can pass myself off as normal, ordinary and unremarkable will fizzle and die. He'll meet Victoria, the sanest, safest person in my so-called life, and he'll see a plump, giggling woman in a furry black wig, and he'll skate right out of here as fast as he can. I can't risk it.

Carter has sorted the wheelie bins, and begins clunking up the path towards the house. I pinch myself, wishing I could wake up and say it was all a nightmare. It is, but sadly I'm not waking up any time soon.

I creep out on to the landing and lean over the banisters. Kevin Carter is in my dad's hall, telling a woman in a silver minidress that he's a very good friend of Jude Reilly.

'That's nice,' says the woman, who has clearly never heard of me. 'Who have you come as, anyway? Blonde, pre-teen Elvis on Rollerblades?'

She offers him the basket of wigs and sunglasses, and obediently he removes his beanie hat and pulls on a black-quiffed wig and shades. He edges past the silver-mini woman and on into the house. I can't bear it. I want to scream, shout and drag him out of there by his black nylon wig. What do I do? Barricade myself in my room and hide under the bed until he's gone, or march downstairs and chuck him out as the gatecrasher he most certainly is?

I see a blue tinsel wig lying discarded on the landing, and the glimmer of an idea starts to form. I drag it on, glancing in the landing mirror. I look like a pale-faced Martian with blue tinsel hair. My own dad wouldn't know me.

I stomp downstairs and grab Kevin Carter by the sleeve of his hoodie.

'What are you doing here?' I demand. 'This is a private party!'

'I was just looking for you,' he grins.

'But you don't know me,' I glower. 'You've never *met* me before.'

'Haven't I?' Carter asks, looking baffled.

'No. I am a complete, total stranger.'

'Right,' says Carter. 'You're definitely not Jude Reilly, then?'

'Definitely not.'

He grins, shrugs and offers me a carton of full-fat milk and a crumpled selection box. 'I guess I'm a gatecrasher, then,' he admits. 'But I brought these for you. To say Happy New Year.'

I put the milk down on the kitchen counter and frown at the selection box. The box has been opened at one end, and when I look more closely it's clear that half the chocolate bars are missing.

'My little brother got to it before me,' Carter says, sadly.

'You have to go,' I tell him.

'I only just got here!'

'And now it's time to go.'

I turn him round and propel him along the hallway, which takes longer than you'd think because of the Rollerblades and the crowds of party people clogging the place up. As he clumps out over the doorstep, a gang of non-Elvis guests burst into the hall, laughing. Posh, Becks, Jordan, Marilyn Monroe and an assortment of Santas – friends of Dad's from the Lookalike Agency, obviously.

'Things are just hotting up,' Carter protests.

'So let's cool them down,' I say firmly. 'I don't know you. You don't know me. You can't just barge into other people's parties. OK?'

Carter pauses by the gate.

'Do I get a New Year's kiss?' he pleads.

'No way! Just push off!'

'Jude,' he says, tugging at the blue tinsel wig. 'I know it's you.'

'I don't know anyone called Jude,' I tell him.

'OK. Whatever. I just wanted to see you, and say Happy New Year.' He takes off the Elvis wig and the shades, and gives them to me. I bite my lip as the lamplight shines on his floppy blonde hair and hazel eyes, and before I see it coming he leans forward and plants a tiny kiss on the tip of my nose. Then he pulls on his beanie hat and skates away, and I'm left standing at the gate alone in a polka-dot dress and a blue tinsel wig.

Behind me, the door bursts open and a sea of people surge out into the street, squealing and laughing and counting down the bells.

'Ten, nine, eight, seven, six . . .'

'Five, four, three, two, one . . .'

'HAPPY NEW YEAR!'

There's an orgy of snogs and hugs and Dad and Victoria scoop me up in a big cuddle, and everyone is laughing and dancing and singing 'Auld Lang Syne'. I join hands with Marilyn Monroe and GI Elvis and my wig slips off and I let myself be pushed about in a big crowd of loud, warm, happy revellers. I think of Gran and Grandad, tucked up in bed at home, and Mum, who'll be out on the razz with Giovanni or Sue.

I wish for a good year, a happy year, for all of us.

As the crowd breaks up and heads back into the house, I look over my shoulder and I'm almost certain I can see a lanky figure standing in the shadows further along the road. I wave into the darkness, and the figure waves back, then turns and skates away.

My mum is behaving very strangely. OK, that's nothing new – she has always been a little odd, but this is different. It's the kind of strange that makes me feel edgy and nervous, like something's wrong, something I don't even want to think about.

She's happy, at least. She has dyed her hair auburn and bought herself a clutch of skimpy frocks in the January sales, and she's out just about every night. Sometimes it's Sue or Giovanni, but mostly it's others, people I don't know so well. She comes in late, then sits up watching *The Wizard of Oz* or playing sad Irish songs on the piano before sneaking up to bed at four or five in the morning. Twice, now, she's been late for work, even though she doesn't start till lunchtime. I don't like it.

I know what's happening, you see, because it's happened before, and the pattern is the same each time. Mum goes out a lot, but not with Sue or Giovanni. She stays out late, then sits up all night and sleeps all day. She stops going to work. Finally, her party mood seems to crash, and she starts staying in, alone, depressed and miserable.

'The doctor says it's a virus,' she says now, talking to Sue on the phone. 'Could be that Asian flu. Every bode id by body aches.' Her voice is a hoarse whisper, and she's holding her nose as she speaks, to produce a muffled, bunged-up effect.

'Baybe toborrow?' she says into the mouthpiece. 'Or the day after, to be od the safe side. Dote wat to pass it od to the customers. I'b sorry, Sue. Yes, of course I'll take care. A couple of days id bed and I'll be fightig fit again.'

She puts the phone down, grinning.

'I hardly ever throw a sickie, do I?' she says to me, without the fake snuffly voice. 'I just need a couple of days' rest.'

'Whatever,' I say, my voice cold.

'I *am* feeling a bit under the weather,' she appeals. 'It might be flu, for all I know . . .'

Or it might be a hangover.

I know I should tell Grandad what I'm thinking, but I look at his familiar, white-bearded face and I can't, I just can't. He has enough to worry about, looking after Gran. Instead, I make pasta shells with cheese sauce for tea, and chop a bit of tinned ham into the sauce. Everyone tucks in, except for Mum, who picks at hers listlessly.

'Not hungry, Rose?' Grandad asks, chirpily.

'Not if this is the best you can do,' she snaps. 'Tastes like rubber.'

My face flames. I look down at my plate. The pasta *is* like rubber, the cheese sauce is lumpy, the bits of ham are cold and stringy. It is the best I can do, but Mum's right, it's not good enough.

'Rose!' Grandad snaps. 'What's got into you? Jude made the dinner, and very good it is too!'

'Well, good for Jude,' Mum says, scraping her chair back from the table. 'I'll see you later. I'm going out.'

She grabs a jacket and slams out of the house.

'Oh dear,' Grandad says, frowning. 'Take no notice, Jude. She's not been eating properly. It's bound to make her snippy. Watching her weight again, I suppose.'

Mum, who is sparrow-skinny at the best of times, does not need to diet, but when she's drinking she loses interest in food. Grandad knows this as well as I do, but he is choosing not to mention it. Like me, he wants another month or so of pretending everything's fine. We are kidding ourselves. We are experts at it.

'Lovely dinner,' Gran says kindly as we wash up together at the sink. 'Was it chicken?'

'Pasta with cheese and ham,' I sigh. 'Not one of my best efforts.'

'It was very nice,' Gran repeats. 'You can't go wrong with chicken.'

'Mum's drinking again,' I say to her, and although my voice is no more than a whisper, I think I see Gran's blue eyes flicker with pain. Sometimes, she knows what's happening. Sometimes, her mind is clear as ice. It's just that it doesn't stay that way. The fog crowds back in, hiding reality, confusing things.

More than anything, I'd like to turn the clock back to when Gran was well, when she could make anything better just by putting her arms round me and stroking my hair. I want to be looked after, but I'm the one who does the looking after, these days.

Gran dries a plate and tries to put it away in the cutlery drawer.

'I love you,' I tell her.

She just smiles, and says, 'I know.'

One evening towards the end of January, I'm hunting through the washing basket in the bathroom, trying to find my blue pyjama top. Instead, I find a small plastic bottle of ginger beer, hidden away among the old socks and cardies, and a shiver slides down my spine. I sink down on to the edge of the bath, cradling the bottle in my hands.

Mum walks into the bathroom, whistling 'Over the Rainbow', getting ready to go out. She peers into the mirror above the sink, dabbing on foundation, stroking on wings of smoky-grey shadow above her eyes.

'OK, Jude?' she asks. 'Which lippy, pet? The red or the pink?'

I ignore her question. 'What's this?' I ask, holding out the plastic bottle. 'I found it in the washing basket.'

Mum swivels round. She looks dismayed, but masks it quickly with a grin and a shrug.

'Just ginger beer,' she says lightly. 'Must have left it in here by accident.' Her perfectly manicured hand reaches out to take the bottle from me, but I unscrew the lid quickly. It smells like ginger beer, mostly. But not quite.

'Jude, don't!' Mum shrieks.

'Why not, if it's just ginger beer?' I argue. But I know why. When the ginger liquid touches my lips, I jump like I've been scalded. There's whisky in there, along with the ginger. I drop the bottle into the bath, watch the brown liquid seep away.

Mum sits down beside me, snaking an arm around my shoulder.

'It's not what you think,' she pleads. 'Really it's not. OK, so I've had a few drinks lately, I admit it. I've been feeling a bit low, I suppose.'

'Drink's not the answer to that!'

'I know, Jude,' she whispers. 'I know, and I'm going to stop, honestly I am. There's no need to tell your grandad, is there? He has enough to worry about as it is.'

That's true enough. Like me, Grandad knows there's something going on, but he's chosen to ignore it. I can't blame him. I want to ignore it too, keep it secret, like I did when I was little and Mum used to make me promise, hand on heart, not to tell.

'It's just my little treat,' she'd whisper, picking

a bottle of cheap whisky off the shelf in the supermarket. 'We all need a treat now and then, don't we, Jude? What would you like, love?' And she'd let me choose a cream cake or a sherbet dip or a comic, and in return I kept my mouth shut about the whisky.

I'm not so easy to bribe, these days. I know that whisky is not a treat, it's a poison. It makes my mum so ill that every time she goes into hospital the doctors tell her that maybe this time will be the last time.

'I have to tell,' I say now, sadly. 'You know I do, Mum. You can't handle this on your own – look what happened last time.'

Mum slumps forward, burying her face in her hands. 'Jude, please!' she appeals. 'I can't let everybody see I've messed up – failed – again. Have you any idea what that feels like?'

I bite my lip. I don't know what it feels like to be Mum, but I know exactly how it feels to be me.

'My life is a mess,' Mum groans. 'Nothing worked out the way I planned it.'

Because of me. She only started drinking heavily after I was born. There's a sad, churny feeling in the pit of my stomach, a prickle of tears behind my eyes.

'It's not so bad, is it?' I ask. 'Mum?'

She laughs, but there's no warmth, no humour in the sound. 'No,' she says. 'It's not so bad.' She smooths down her hair, fixes a shaky smile on her face. 'It's not bad, Jude, but it could be a whole lot better. And it will be. I'm going to be a better mum, a better daughter. Set up my own business, maybe, make you proud of me! We've had some good times, haven't we? Well, I'm going to make sure we have more!'

Good times . . . yeah, we had them, once.

Days at the seaside, eating egg sandwiches gritty with sand, Gran and Grandad paddling in the water and sipping lukewarm tea from a flask while Mum and I built sandcastles, collected shells, slathered ourselves in suntan lotion and floated around on neon-bright lilos. Gran and Grandad would stroll along the prom or mooch around the souvenir shops while Mum and I tried out the scariest rides at the funfair, screaming like crazy, then queuing up for more. We'd all meet up later at a little ice-cream shop, crowding into a window booth to eat ice-cream sundaes before getting the train home.

There haven't been any days like that for a long, long time, not since Gran got ill. It's like she was the one holding us all together, keeping us strong, and once she lost the plot we all fell to bits.

Mum faces me, her eyes wet with tears. 'I know things haven't been easy for you,' she whispers. 'That's why I'm asking you to keep this little slip a secret, give me a chance to stop. Do you think I haven't noticed how tired your grandad is looking these days? He has a full-time job looking after your gran. The last thing he needs is for me to go off the rails again.'

'So don't,' I say in a small, quavery voice. 'Don't, Mum.'

'I won't,' she says, blotting at her tears with a corner of bath towel. 'I won't, I promise. Look – let me prove it!'

She jumps up, dragging me into her bedroom. She roots under the bed to unearth a whisky bottle, almost full, then marches into the bathroom and pours it all down the sink.

'See? I mean it, Jude. I've learned my lesson. Just give me a chance – believe me.'

'I do,' I tell her. 'You're strong – you can do it.'

Mum droops sadly. 'I'm not strong. That's the trouble. And sometimes, a little drink makes me feel like I am – like I can cope – when really it just wrecks everything. I'll put things right, I promise you.'

I bite my lip, nodding slowly, and Mum flings her arms around me in a warm, sweet-smelling hug that chases all my doubts away.

Mum cancels her night out and nips down to the corner shops to buy fish 'n' chips and ice cream. We're just finishing the chips when she brings in a tray of home-made ice-cream sundaes, the little glass dishes piled high with fruit and ice cream, crowned with chocolate sauce and sprinkles.

'Sundaes!' Gran beams over her knitting. 'What a lovely surprise!'

'Yes, thanks, Rose, pet,' Grandad says. 'Delicious!'

I take a mouthful of rich, creamy sundae, shivering at its icy coldness. The chocolate sauce seems too sweet, too sickly, and the fruit isn't quite ripe. Why is nothing ever as perfect as the way I remember it? There's an ice-cream numbness at the back of my throat that feels like sadness.

Mum winks at me. 'Good times,' she whispers. 'Trust me.'

I almost do.

10

Mum spends a whole week tidying the house, dusting, hoovering, polishing every surface. She washes dishes, clothes, curtains, even Toto's stripy blanket. Next, she moves on to ironing. I come home from school to find my wardrobe crammed with crisply ironed shirts and sweatshirts, my shoes polished to a high shine.

I slip on a red T-shirt and skinny jeans, both soft and fragrant with fabric conditioner, and pad down to the living room with my homework. Mum is spritzing the windows with a green spray, wiping away the fog of years.

'Thanks, Mum,' I say, and it's not just for the clothes and the tidying up, it's for staying off the drink. Mum looks round from her polishing and winks.

'Yes, very nice, love,' Grandad agrees. He snaps the braces on his old green cord trousers, which now boast razor-sharp creases front and back. 'Thanks, Rose.'

'Those cords are so old and worn, though.' Mum frowns. 'You need new ones, and Mum needs stuff too – when was the last time she had a new dress? You'd like that, wouldn't you, Mum? Something pretty to wear?'

Gran's eyes sparkle. 'I bought the loveliest dress in town last week,' she says. 'Blue tafetta, it was, with a nipped-in waist and a full-circle skirt.'

'I don't think that was last week,' Mum says gently.

'No, not last week,' Grandad chips in. 'But I remember it as if it were yesterday, Molly, love. You wore that dress to the Locarno, and every young man in the place wanted to dance with you. You wouldn't have anything to do with them – you only had eyes for one lad. Scruffy fella, fresh off the boat from Dublin, in a borrowed suit and shoes with holes in them. You danced with him all night, Molly, and he thought he was the luckiest man alive. He still does.'

'My Patrick,' Gran says softly.

My eyes widen. 'Was that you, Grandad?'

'It was. Your gran looked like an angel in that blue dress, the first night we met.' He turns to the sideboard and rummages through a drawer, unearthing a faded photograph album.

Near the front, held in with a little white triangle in each corner, is a black-and-white picture of a couple, grinning at the camera. The young man looks cute and cheeky, his hair sticking up untidily, his suit too big for him. The girl is beautiful, breathless, her face shining with love and confidence like she hasn't a care in the world. She has masses of black, wavy hair tied up in a high ponytail, and her lips are parted in a big, happy grin.

I study those faces hard, but I can't see much trace of Gran and Grandad there. They are like shadows from another world.

'Crazy quiff,' Mum says, peering over my shoulder. 'I'd forgotten you were a rock 'n' roller, Dad! And this is Mum's famous dress . . .'

The girl in the picture is wearing a shimmery, off-the-shoulder dress that hugs her figure and flares out from her tiny waist to just below the knees. It looks like a special dress, a dress for dancing, for falling in love.

'It was peacock blue,' Grandad says. 'The exact same shade as her eyes.'

I look at Gran now and my heart aches for the way time has changed her. What happened to the young girl in the picture, dancing the night away? Or even the cuddly, capable Gran who read me bedtime stories, taught me to make apple pie and once showed Nuala and me how to hand-jive to one of Dad's Elvis CDs? We were seven and she was sixty-six, and she was still dancing and laughing, her skirt swishing out around her, long after Nuala and I had given up.

'Remember that night, Molly?' Grandad asks now, showing her the photograph. 'The blue tafetta dress?'

Gran frowns, squinting at the picture as though she can't quite see it clearly. 'Do we know these people?' she asks, and I have to turn away because I can't bear to watch any more.

On Saturday, just before tea, Mum arrives home in a taxi, laden with carrier bags. The driver has to help her up the path with them, and she gives him a fiver tip.

'What's going on, Rose, love?' Grandad asks. 'What is all this?'

'Wait and see!' Mum announces, dumping the bags in the living room. 'I've been shopping. It was all in the sales, before you ask!'

From one bag, she pulls out a cornflower-blue button-through dress with a gathered skirt, and Gran drops her knitting and stands up shakily, her mouth making a perfect 'o' shape.

'Do you like it?' Mum wants to know. 'What do you think?'

Gran hugs the dress to her, then hugs Mum. 'It's beautiful!' she whispers. There's a peacock-blue cardigan too, soft and fluffy, and a blue silky scarf and a new brushed cotton nightie. Gran's face is aglow with pleasure.

'I didn't forget you, Dad,' Mum says, dropping a couple of carrier bags at Grandad's feet. 'Or you, Jude, sweetheart!'

It's like everyone's birthday and Christmas has come at once. Grandad has new cord trousers, a zip-up pullover with leather patches on the elbows, a checked shirt and a pair of braces. I get new jeans, a mohair sweater, tartan jammies and a pair of pink Converse trainers. Mum fishes around in the last carrier bag and brings out a squeaky dog chew, which she throws to Toto. He falls on it in a frenzy of crimped hair and excitement, squeaking madly. Everybody loves their prezzies, and Mum basks in our delight.

'These can't have been in the sales, Mum,' I exclaim, trying on the trainers. 'They're fantastic!'

'It's too much, Rose, love,' Grandad says, anxiously. 'Too much.'

'Can't I buy a couple of little treats for my family?' Mum asks, and I frown at the word 'treats' because in my mind it doesn't mean clothes or squeaky dog toys, but something forbidden, something bad. I glance at Mum. Her good mood is down to a mad shopping spree, nothing else. I hope.

'You deserve it, don't you?' Mum continues. 'We all do! What are credit cards for?'

She sees the anxious look on Grandad's face and jumps in. 'Don't worry, Dad. I'm working, aren't I? I'll pay it back.' She looks at him and smiles. 'Don't you like your stuff?'

'Of course I do!' Grandad says. 'Thank you, Rose, love. You're a good girl.'

'Yeah, thanks, Mum,' I add. 'I love it all.'

The clothes are brilliant, but the best thing of all is having a mum who acts like a mum – a mum who isn't drinking. A mum who keeps her promises.

'Soft, so soft,' Gran is whispering, stroking her fluffy cardigan.

'So, did you get anything for yourself?' I ask, eyeing the last carrier bag. 'Let's see!'

Mum gets all brisk suddenly, gathering up her bag. 'Just a couple of tops, that's all,' she says, flashing me a wisp of pink and turquoise. 'I'll show you later, OK? I'm going out with some of the girls tonight.'

'Oh . . . OK.' Mum hasn't been out all week, but I guess she can't stay in forever, drinking or not.

'That's OK with you all, isn't it?' she asks, an edge of challenge in her voice. 'One night out with my mates? I won't be late.'

'No, no, that's fine, Rose, love,' Grandad echoes. 'You get out and enjoy yourself.' I can see a shadow of doubt fall over his face, and I know what it is because I feel it too.

'Well, just going to get ready,' Mum announces, edging past me with the carrier bag swinging. As she walks up the stairs, I hear the clink of bottles, clear as day. Underneath the wispy pink and turquoise tops there is something hidden, something heavy, something made of glass.

One week, that's all she lasted. One week of housework and presents and hugs, and now it's over. There's a sour taste in my mouth, the taste of disappointment. I fell for it again, the lies, the promises – just like I always do.

Is that all I'm worth, a few days' effort, a new pair of trainers, an ice-cream sundae?

Stupid, stupid, stupid.

'Have you ever really fancied a boy?' Nuala O'Sullivan asks. 'You know, a *real* boy? Not counting Orlando Bloom or David Beckham or the Mousset brothers?'

The Mousset brothers, Yassain, Youssuf and Khalid, run the corner shop next to St Joseph's. They are very cool and very gorgeous, and every girl pupil is madly in love with them. They will all be millionaires sometime soon, based on sky-high sales of bubblegum and cherry cola.

'No,' I say firmly. 'Boys are a waste of time.'

'So, you don't have a crush on Kevin Carter?' Nuala persists.

'Me? No way!' I protest, turning beetroot at the thought. 'Why? Do you?'

The idea of Nuala and Kevin makes me feel all hot and prickly. It's not a nice feeling. I'm not sure why – if Nuala and Kevin got together, he'd stop stalking me, wouldn't he? Problem solved. Well, one of them.

'No, silly,' Nuala scoffs. 'Why would I fancy him? Seriously, Jude, he's more your type.'

'Thanks a bunch.'

'And *he* fancies *you*,' Nuala continues. 'Don't think I haven't noticed. He's besotted, totally. Lost the plot. The poor lad had detention, yesterday, for chucking paper planes at you in maths. He is *desperate* for your attention.'

'You think so?'

'Oh, come on, Jude!' Nuala laughs. 'Take pity on the boy! Either tell him to back off or give him a chance. Have you no heart?'

''Course I have!'

'Well, it must be made of ice,' Nuala huffs. 'Poor Carter.'

Poor Carter?

'He's been talking to you!' I exclaim. 'What's he said?'

'Nothing!' Nuala protests. 'He just happened to ask me for your phone number . . .'

'Nuala! Please tell me you didn't . . .'

'It's just a phone number . . .'

I slump, thinking of what might happen if Carter rings and gets chatting to Gran about knitting patterns, or Grandad about Gaelic football, or Mum about whether whisky is a treat or a curse.

'Nuala, I don't want a boyfriend,' I say. 'My life is complicated enough.'

'A boyfriend would be a *nice* complication,' she says. 'I wouldn't mind, if someone fancied me.'

'You might, if it was Kevin Carter,' I tell her.

'Well. Maybe.'

That night, I camp out near the phone just in case Carter rings.

Mum has slipped back into the same old pattern of late nights and sulky sleep-ins. While I wait, there's a call from Sue, asking why Mum wasn't in work this afternoon, one from Giovanni, asking why Mum didn't turn up for their date last night, and one from a double-glazing company, asking us to put in UPVC windows at a bargain, never-to-be-repeated price.

It is so typical of a boy to ask for your number and not bother to ring. I begin to feel quite huffy.

'Expecting a call?' Grandad asks.

'No,' I snap. 'Why would I be?'

'Just wondered.'

It's almost ten when he finally rings, and Grandad beats me to the phone. 'Some idiot waffling on about boxing,' he grumbles. 'For you.'

I drag the phone out into the hall, and sit on the stairs.

'You're avoiding me,' Carter says. 'You've been avoiding me since New Year. Nuala says it's because you're shy.'

'I am not shy!' I protest.

'No? I thought not. A girl who can wear a blue tinsel wig and a polka-dot minidress can't really be shy. It looked like a good party.'

'It was,' I admit. The kiss on the nose bit was a highlight, but I'm not about to tell him that.

'Nuala says you have a problem with trusting boys, because your mum and dad split up,' Carter goes on.

'Oh? Nuala says quite a lot, doesn't she?' I snap. 'Wouldn't you be better off with her?'

'She's not my type,' Carter says.

'So what is your type?'

'Tall, skinny, black hair, blue eyes, freckly nose. Blue tinsel wig and snowflakes optional.'

'Skinny?' I squeal.

'Definitely. Pretending to be shy, sensible and stand-offish when really you're mad about me.'

'You sure about that?'

'No, but I'm hoping.'

'Carter, I have to go now,' I tell him.

'You can call me Kevin.'

'Bye, Carter.'

I put the phone down. I am mad at Nuala for saying I have a problem trusting boys. I don't. I have a problem trusting *anyone* I'm not related to, plus quite a few people I am. What's wrong with that?

Life is complicated enough, especially right

now. Carter wouldn't understand. He'd laugh, or worse, he'd feel sorry for me, and I don't need that. I don't need *him*.

There's a scuffling noise out on the front doorstep, and I open the door. Mum falls into the hallway, unsteadily. The side of her coat is torn and grey with dirt, her tights are ripped and the heel of her right shoe is broken.

'Mum! Oh, Mum, what's happened? Grandad! Quick!'

Grandad comes into the hall, his face ashen.

'Rose, pet, whatever's happened?' he asks, taking her arm, helping her out of her coat. 'Did somebody try to hurt you?'

'Hurt me?' Mum slurs. 'No, of course not. Stop fussing. I slipped over on the ice. No problem. Could have happened to anyone.'

She totters into the living room, flopping down on to the sofa. I bring her a coffee and she takes it sulkily, sipping some and spilling the rest. We pretend not to notice.

Mum fell over on the ice, and yes, it could have happened to anyone, but it happened to her. Because she was drunk.

I go back to my homework, chewing my lip. We don't stand up to Mum when she's drinking. We ignore it until we can't ignore it any longer, because we don't know what to do, how to cope, how to help her. We stay silent and pretend it's not happening, because nothing will stop her, short of a week in the hospital, and she's not ill enough for that yet.

The last time this happened I was ten, and it was the worst six months of my life. Nobody could get through to her – not me, not Gran, Grandad or Giovanni. She drank until her liver couldn't cope any more. The alcohol poisoned her body, turning her skin yellow, bloating her body. Even the whites of her eyes were the colour of custard. She collapsed in the house and an ambulance took her to hospital, and when some kid at school said they'd seen her carried out on a stretcher, I told everyone she had a rare blood disease, and that she might die.

It wasn't exactly a lie.

My mum is an alcoholic, and Grandad says it's a disease, an addiction. It's in her blood. Unless she stops drinking it will kill her, one day – that's what the doctors say. Already, she has destroyed some parts of her liver, damaged her heart. She's damaged mine, I know that much.

I wasn't brave enough to tell the kids at school the truth – not even Nuala. They wouldn't have understood. They'd have felt sorry for me, because my own mum doesn't love me enough to kick the drink. She'd rather drink herself to death, slowly, having a few laughs along the way.

Grandad sits down, hiding behind the newspaper, trying to read, hands shaking. Gran keeps knitting, a rainbow-striped scarf that's quite new, just a metre long. Her knitting needles click quietly, and the tears slip down her face in silence, almost as though she knows what's going on.

On Valentine's Day, Giovanni arrives on the doorstep at eight in the morning with an armful of red roses and a box of chocolates for Mum. She is still in bed.

'Tell her I'm taking her for a special day out,' Giovanni grins, gesturing towards the ice-cream van parked skew-whiff on the kerb. 'We will go to the seaside and walk hand in hand along the beach, eat tiramisu at the best Italian restaurant I know, dance until the early hours and then kiss beneath the stars.'

'Yeuch, Giovanni, too much information.' I shudder, stomping off up the stairs to try and wake Mum. The room smells of whisky and stale smoke. I spot a clutch of old fag ends in a makeshift saucer ashtray and a crumpled cigarette packet on the bedside table. My heart thumps. She gave up smoking two years ago.

Tears sting my eyes, but I blink them back. Mum is curled up beneath the covers, clutching a plastic bottle that says it's ginger beer but almost certainly isn't. I tug back the blankets and shake her shoulders gently, but she swats me off like I'm some kind of annoying insect.

'Mum,' I hiss. 'Wake up. It's Valentine's Day, and Giovanni is here with flowers and chocolates. He's taking you for a special day out.'

Giovanni knows about Mum's problem. The last time she was ill, he visited her in hospital, brought her flowers, drove her in the ratty old ice-cream van to the AA meetings that helped her stay off the drink afterwards. He knows what she's like at her worst – he must have noticed what's going on now, surely?

'Tell him to get lost,' Mum says, grumpily. 'I'm asleep.'

'Then wake *up*,' I tell her. 'Come on, Mum, he's made a real effort. You'll enjoy it – a day at the seaside, a romantic dinner for two. It'll cheer you up.'

'I don't *need* cheering up,' Mum snaps, dragging the blankets back so she can burrow back down. 'Tell him to go away.'

At that moment, the chimes of the ice-cream van start to play at full volume. I pull back the curtains to look out of the window, and there's Giovanni, leaning on the gate, waving. Gran, Grandad and Toto wander out on to the garden

81

path, and Giovanni serves them all an early morning ice-cream cornet, adorned with nuts and raspberry sauce.

'Come on, Rosa, bella!' Giovanni shouts up to the window. 'Wake up! Come away with me, for a life of love, romance and ice-cream sundaes!'

I let the curtain drop before anyone can see me. Isn't it bad enough to have relatives that are seriously weird without them attracting whole shedloads of loopy hangers-on? Why can't Mum date someone normal, a bloke who wears Next suits and shiny shoes and doesn't wake up the whole neighbourhood on Valentine's morning with wailing ice-cream sirens and declarations of love?

'What's he playing at?' Mum scowls, crawling out of bed, bleary-eyed, hair sticking up in all directions like a backcombed, auburn scarecrow. She drags back the curtain and flings the window open.

'Ciao, bella,' Giovanni calls, blowing Mum a kiss.

'Giovanni, just get lost!' she shouts. 'I'm not interested, OK?'

'Mum!' I protest. 'Don't! People will hear!'

She takes no notice, leaning out of the window and waving her fist. I notice she's wearing nothing but a lime-green satin slip, trimmed with pink lace, and I want to die of shame.

'Go on,' she roars at Giovanni. 'Get lost! Take the hint! Take your stinking roses and your fancy chocolates and that heap of junk you call a van and leave me alone. OK?'

She slams the window shut and stomps past me in a cloud of whisky fumes, flinging herself down on the bed.

'As if I'd waste my time with a no-hoper like that,' she mutters, snuggling under the blankets. 'I have better things to do with my time.'

I can see that. She reaches out for the ginger-beer bottle and unscrews the lid, taking a few swigs of watery brown liquid, then fumbles for a cigarette. She produces an ancient silver lighter and flicks it a couple of times, lighting up.

Well hey, who would want a life of love, romance and ice-cream sundaes when you can settle for smoking and drinking yourself to death? It's obvious.

Giovanni is still there as I grab my bag and leave for school, serving cornets to a knot of neighbourhood kids and talking to Grandad.

'She didn't mean it,' Giovanni is saying. 'I know she didn't. Perhaps I handled it wrong?'

'It's not you, Giovanni,' Grandad says, shaking his head. 'It's the drink.'

Giovanni shrugs. 'What can I do? I love her,

but she needs help. I have to let her see that she can't drive me away.'

Grandad scratches his head. 'Maybe,' he says. 'But I'd stay out of her way for a while, son. I'm sorry.'

'Want a lift to school?' Giovanni calls as I slip past the crowd of kids slurping at their breakfast cornets.

'Er, no thanks, Giovanni,' I tell him. 'I – um – I have a bus pass.'

The thought of arriving at school in a rusty old ice-cream van is enough to make me feel faint.

'A cornet, then?' Giovanni suggests. 'Extra nuts and sauce?'

'OK, thanks.' I reach up for the ice-cream cone and try not to worry about being seen eating ice cream in February. Lots of people do, I expect. Especially around here, this morning.

'Sorry about Mum,' I say. Giovanni may not be who *I'd* pick for Mum, but he's a nice bloke and he loves her. He is kind and thoughtful, and doesn't complain when Toto sniffs his trousers.

'She breaks my heart,' Giovanni declares, pulling a dramatic face and striking his chest with his fist.

I know how he feels. She breaks mine too.

*

I am half expecting Carter to appear from behind a dustbin or skate up as I wait at the bus stop, but there's no sign of him. Perhaps he doesn't even know it's Valentine's Day. Perhaps he isn't the card-sending sort of boy, or maybe he's finally got the message and given up hope. He's probably canoodling at the school gates with Kristina Kowalski right now.

Boys are so fickle.

At the school gates, though, there is no sign of Carter, or Kristina Kowalski. I hook up with Nuala in the playground.

'So, did you get a card from Carter?' she demands. 'Hearts, flowers, fluffy bunnies?'

'No,' I snap. 'Like I care, anyhow. Valentine's Day is just a load of commercial rubbish. And besides, I do *not* like Kevin Carter.'

Nuala smirks. I hate it when she does that.

When we get to our form room, Kristina Kowalski is perched on a desk at the back, clutching an armful of padded, fluffy, outsized cards and fluttering her eyelashes.

'I don't know *why* I've got so many,' she simpers to an admiring audience. 'Boys just seem to like me. I guess I'm just a popular girl. I don't know why!'

I roll my eyes. Kristina is wearing hipsters today, slung so low you can see the back of her thong peeking out over the top. Her white shirt is tight, short and scarily see-through. A silver belly-clip glints at her navel, drawing attention to her flat, brown tummy. Boys gawp at Kristina, bug-eyed, but of course, she doesn't know why.

When Brendan Coyle saunters in and slaps her on the bum, she just giggles and tosses her hair and wiggles over to where he's sitting for more of the same. Nuala makes puking noises behind her hand, and I notice with relief that Kevin Carter is sitting alone in the corner of the room, busy with some homework. He wouldn't fall for a girl like Kristina. Would he?

There's something stuck to the seat of my chair. I edge over to investigate, and find a small, pink Love Hearts sweetie with *Hot lips* written on it. It's stuck down with Blu-tack, and I have to prise it off, carefully. I can't help glancing over at Carter. He's still engrossed in his homework, but he's smiling.

There's a pale green sweetie that says *My girl* stuck to my desktop. I'm grinning as I pick it up, and Nuala raises an eyebrow.

'Don't like him, eh?' she whispers, as Miss Devlin sweeps into the form room and starts rattling through the register.

After games, I find Love Hearts sweets in each

of my boots, as well as in the pockets of my school blazer.

'How did he *do* that?' Nuala asks. 'Get into the girls' changing room? He must really like you.'

'They're just sweets,' I tell her.

'No, Jude, they're valentines,' she corrects me. 'They're clever, cute and resourceful. Admit it.'

I pull a face. 'I can't exactly eat them,' I complain. 'These two had Blu-tack on them, these were in my boots . . .'

'You're not supposed to *eat* them,' Nuala sighs. 'You're supposed to treasure them forever. What's wrong with you?'

'Nothing!' I protest, as a sweetie saying *Wild thing* drops out of the pages of my French book.

Nuala thinks my heart is made of ice, but the ice is melting, very slowly, and just around the edges. It's a scary feeling.

In the dinner hall, I open my lunch box to find *Trust me* stuck to the inside lid, and a scattering of other messages strewn in among my cheese-and-pickle sandwiches. Carter, munching happily on a chip roll, winks as he strolls past me.

In art, I find Love Hearts sweets in my folder, inside my sketchbook, in my pencil case. 'They're like little badges,' Nuala says, stroking the pastel-coloured sweets. 'Hey! Why don't you wear them as badges? Wear your heart on your sleeve?'

'No way!' I protest. 'People would see!'

'And?' Nuala shrugs.

'And they'd want to know, and . . . it'd be embarrassing.'

'Does Carter look embarrassed?' Nuala demands.

'No, but . . .'

'Go on,' she teases. 'Live a little!'

She asks Mr Latimer if she can use the glue gun, and together we stick the Love Hearts sweeties all over my black canvas school bag. It looks cool.

'Nice idea,' Carter says as we walk down to the bus stops. 'Sticking them all over your bag. I'm glad you like them.'

'You're not meant to admit it was you,' I tell him.

'Aren't I? Does that mean I'm not allowed to ask you out, either?'

'Carter, no way,' I say, panicked. I stop mid-stride and let the crowds of people stream on past. 'You can't ask me out, not ever. I'm not the dating kind. I . . . I think you're wasting your time with me.'

Carter looks at me. 'I don't,' he says. 'Can I walk you home?'

'I've got piano practice.'

'So, can I walk you to piano practice?'

I shake my head. 'This is not going to work,' I tell him.

'Sure it is.' Carter laughs. 'You worry too much.'

He sits down on the grass and pulls his skates out of his rucksack, dragging them on. I turn and walk away.

'Hey, wait,' Carter calls, but I break into a run and jump on to a bus for the city centre just as it pulls away from the kerb. As I push through the scrum of uniformed teenagers, I glance back through the window and see Carter, skating after the bus, waving.

At piano practice, Miss Lloyd leaves me to set my books out and run through my scales while she fixes herself a cup of coffee. I open my Grade Four book at my first piece, and a small, pale-yellow sweetie drops out, landing on the piano keys.

I love u.

I am standing in the bedroom at Dad and Victoria's place, wearing a sugar-pink minidress and a scowl.

'Shorter?' Victoria wants to know. 'You've got good legs, Jude.'

'No, no, it's fine,' I insist. This is a lie, but then again, a sugar-pink bridesmaid's dress is never going to be fine, no matter what length it is.

Victoria shrugs and starts pinning a length of red tassel trim round the hem. 'Red winkle-picker boots and a red hairband . . . you'll look amazing!' she declares.

I bite my lip and try hard to smile.

Surprise, surprise, Dad and Victoria are having a 1960s wedding. 'We'll do your hair all backcombed, Jude, with that flick-up thing round the edge like we did for the New Year's party,' Victoria is saying. 'It's just the tights we need, now. White or pink? What d'you think?'

'I don't mind,' I tell her. I don't. Either way, I'll look disgusting.

Victoria is getting married in the black beehive wig and a white minidress with a huge, frothy veil, white crinkly knee-boots and white lacy tights. Dad is going to wear a custom-made white satin catsuit with a silver lurex collar and cape, and, of course, blue suede shoes. Beside them, I will look almost normal.

'It's so-o-o exciting!' Victoria squeals, securing the last pin and steering me towards the mirror. I catch a glimpse of pink above white legs and knobbly knees, and shut my eyes quickly.

'I'll carry pink roses, and you'll carry white,' she gabbles on. 'We'll complement each other. We're going to have "Love Me Tender" instead of the wedding march, too!'

'That's cool, Victoria,' I say, through gritted teeth. Victoria and Dad are happy, planning their big day. They've already shown me pictures of Las Vegas, USA, where you can get married in a tacky chapel of lurve with an Elvis preacher to perform the ceremony. Scary. Luckily for me, their savings do not stretch to a Las Vegas wedding.

'It doesn't matter about Las Vegas,' Victoria tells me later, as the three of us curl up beside the gas fire with mugs of tea. 'Gretna Green is just as romantic, and all our friends can be with us too.'

'Gretna Green?' I echo.

'That's right.' Dad grins. 'The famous Old Smithy at Gretna Green, just over the border in Scotland! In the past, English teenagers used to run away to Gretna to get married, because the Scottish laws were different back then, and they could get married without their parents' consent!'

'You're forty-five!' I point out.

'Well, yes,' Dad admits. 'Obviously. I mean, we'd just be doing it for the romance factor.'

I roll my eyes. At least Gretna Green is a long, long way from Coventry. The chances of anyone from school seeing me in my 1960s puke-pink mini are almost nil.

'Just wait till you hear what your dad has planned for the honeymoon,' Victoria says. 'Tell her, Bobby!'

Dad produces a glossy brochure with a weirdo-pink car on the front. He has hired a 1950s pink Cadillac to take them up to Gretna Green, and then on for a tour through the Highlands of Scotland. They will stop off at social clubs and old folks' homes in Killiekrankie, Glencoe, Inverness, Stirling and Perth for a whistle-stop series of Elvis gigs.

'It'll be a sort of working honeymoon,' he tells me. 'Rock 'n' rollin' by night, cruising along single-track roads and through heather-clad hills by day. Watch out, Scotland, here we come!'

I study the brochure, taking in the shiny chrome and pointy pink tail fins. This car looks like it was designed by a deranged child with a Barbie fixation. 'Right,' I say. 'And you think the pink Cadillac will be up to the single-track roads and heather-clad hills? It being fifty-odd years old and all that?'

Dad frowns. 'Of course it will,' he says gruffly. 'Those classic cars were built to last. You'll see, anyway – you can drive up to Gretna Green with us. We'll have the works – a sixties karaoke and bagpipes and fireworks, the lot. Keep your diary free for the first of April!'

'The . . . what?'

'April the first.' Dad grins. 'Thought it'd be a bit of a laugh! April Fool's Day!'

'The date fitted,' Victoria explains. 'We wanted a spring wedding, and all the later Saturdays were busy. There were gaps for April the first. Some people don't fancy getting married that day, apparently.'

'I wonder why?' I mutter.

'It's funny, Jude,' Dad insists. 'A day to remember. Think about it – we'll never be able to forget our anniversary, will we?' He leans over to kiss Victoria on the cheek, then winks at me.

I sip my tea, wondering if I am the only sane person in my entire family. Looks like it.

*

An invitation to Dad and Victoria's wedding appears. The card is shaped like a profile of Elvis, with a curling lip and a quiff made of black fur fabric. Mum, making a rare pre-lunchtime appearance at the breakfast table, picks it up distastefully, as though it may be carrying germs.

'Bobby and Victoria would like to invite Patrick, Molly and Jude to celebrate their wedding at 11.30 on Saturday 1 April at the Old Smithy, Gretna Green, and to the reception afterwards at the Thistle Hotel and Diner. 1950s/60s attire optional. For goodness' sake! How tacky is that!' she exclaims. 'And they haven't even had the courtesy to invite me!'

'Rose, pet, you wouldn't want to go to Bobby's wedding, now, would you?' Grandad reasons.

'I shouldn't think that any of you would want to go,' Mum says, stubbing out her ciggy on a side plate. 'Out of loyalty to me.'

'Well, now, I don't suppose Molly and I *will* go,' Grandad admits. 'It's too far for Molly. All that travelling – she's not really up to it. Nice of them to think of us, though.'

'Nice?' Mum barks. '*Nice?* Really!'

'But *you* left Bobby,' Grandad points out. 'Not the other way round, Rose. It's good that he's found someone else, settling down at last.'

'I always knew it would work out in the end,' Gran says dreamily. 'Perhaps I'll get a new hat.

You'll need a new suit, Patrick, to walk our Rose down the aisle.'

'It's not *my* wedding,' Mum says scornfully. 'Thank goodness.'

Gran's face crumples. 'But I thought . . . ?'

'Bobby's marrying Victoria,' Grandad reminds her. 'You remember, Molly, love.'

'Oh. Well, you missed your chance there, Rose, pet,' Gran says. 'Never mind. Perhaps you'll catch the bouquet?'

Mum snorts. 'As if. Who wants to get married anyway? I'm a career girl.'

'I thought you were a hairdresser!' Gran says, baffled.

Mum rolls her eyes, lighting another cigarette and frowning at the invitation. 'Have you seen the date? April Fool's Day! Well, that's the biggest joke of all, isn't it?'

There's a dull silence, broken only by the clickety-click of Gran's knitting.

'It won't last,' Mum says darkly, giving her toast and jam to Toto and stomping upstairs to bed. 'If Sue rings, tell her I'm feeling under the weather,' she calls down to us. 'I'm going to take a couple of days off, get a proper rest. Sue knows how hard I work. She'll understand.'

Maybe, maybe not.

After school, I get home to find Mum has recovered enough to get dressed up and style her hair ready to head off to town to meet some friends.

'Which friends, pet?' Grandad asks. 'Where will you be? Don't be too late, now!'

'Late?' Mum laughs harshly. 'What am I, sixteen again? I'll come home when I want to, Dad. You don't know my friends, and we don't know yet where we'll be, so just back off. Is it a crime to go out once in a while? Have a little drink, relax, have fun?'

Gran and Grandad look at her, silent. Their eyes are very blue, very shiny, their faces are pale and crinkly and sad. They look too old to be coping with this, too old to know what to do.

'I can look after myself,' Mum says now, shrugging on a pink leather jacket with a couple of old ciggy burns on the sleeve. I notice her make-up is streaky, the mascara all smudged and claggy.

'You can't,' I hear myself say. 'You can't look after yourself, or me, or Gran and Grandad. You're smoking again, and you promised you never would. And drinking, even though you swore blind that you'd stop. You don't care about us – all you care about is the next whisky, even though you know it's poisoning you. Can't you see what you're doing, Mum?' I plead.

Mum's eyes flash with anger, and her hand springs up to slap my cheek. Somehow, she pulls back, and her hand hovers in mid-air, shaking. She claps the hand over her mouth, and her whole body seems to shudder.

'How could you understand the things I've been through?' she hisses at me. 'The heartbreak? I bring a wage in, don't I? I've brought you up single-handed, and you've never wanted for a thing. Aren't I still at home looking after those two –' she jerks a finger towards Gran and Grandad – 'even though they're enough to drive anyone mad with their fussing and their nagging? What more do you all want? Oh, you make me sick, the lot of you.'

She shoves her way out of the door, slamming it behind her.

I press a hand to my cheek, almost as though I can feel the slap that never quite happened. My heart is thumping.

'What a very rude girl,' Gran says into the silence. 'No manners at all. I don't think we should ask her here again. In fact, I've a good mind to have a word with her mother.'

'You do that, Molly, love,' Grandad says, and I smile, in spite of everything. Grandad slips an arm round my shoulder, leading me back into the living room.

'She didn't mean it, pet,' he says. 'It's the drink talking. She'd never hurt you, Jude.'

'I just wanted her to know how it feels for us,' I whisper. 'I hate it!'

I look at Grandad's tired eyes, at Gran, hunched in an armchair with her knitting, chewing her lip, tugging holes in the wool with long, anxious fingers. Toto puts his head on her lap, and she strokes his fur, absently.

'We all hate it,' Grandad says.

We're just not allowed to talk about it. We don't know how. I wipe my eyes – there's no way I'm going to cry when Gran and Grandad need me to be strong.

'Anyone hungry?' I ask, too brightly. 'Beans on toast?'

'Lovely, pet.'

So I make beans on toast and Grandad makes a pot of tea, and Gran produces a packet of jammie dodgers from her knitting bag. We are still munching our way through this feast when Sue from the hairdresser's calls round. Sue is plump and chatty, and she's good friends with Mum when Mum isn't drinking. Right now, though, Sue has been replaced by an ever-changing cast of nameless drinking mates, Mum's new best friends for a week, a day, an hour.

I pour Sue a mug of tea and arrange some jammie dodgers on a plate for her.

'Oh, Sue, love, sit down,' Grandad says. I know right away he won't tell her the truth. No one must know.

'I'm sorry Rose didn't make it in to work today,' he says brightly. 'She wasn't feeling too good – she's never quite shaken off that flu since January. Give her a couple of days and she'll be back on top form.'

'I expect she was feeling embarrassed, after yesterday, too,' Sue says, taking the tea and biscuits.

'Yesterday?'

'Well, you know, the accident and everything,' Sue says.

'Yes, of course, I expect so,' Grandad bluffs.

'What accident?' I ask.

Sue looks kind of pink. 'She didn't tell you? Oh, well, it was nothing to worry about. Could have happened to anyone. I just wanted to let her know that it was all sorted out, the client has promised not to go to the papers or anything. I offered her a year's free hairdressing and manicures at the salon . . .'

'Sue,' I say bluntly. 'What happened?'

'Um, well, Rose mixed up a hair colour a little too strong and left the client under the hairdryer for too long . . .'

'And?'

'Well, she dyed Miss Devlin's hair green,' Sue admits. 'With slight burns to the scalp.'

I sink down into an armchair.

'As in Miss Devlin the English teacher?' I ask faintly. 'My form tutor?'

'I think she does teach up at St Joe's, now that you mention it.'

I let out a long, ragged breath. Mum can hardly get her act together to go into work these days, but when she does appear she manages to maim the only teacher at St Joseph's I actually like. Miss Devlin with green hair? It doesn't bear thinking about.

'She was away today,' I recall, horrified. 'We had a cover teacher.'

'Well, it took a while to put things right,' Sue explained. 'She's fine now, apart from the burns, and I put some aloe vera gel on those. We settled for "Golden Sunset" in the end.'

'You dyed Miss Devlin's hair blonde?' I ask. This is almost as shocking as dyeing it green.

'Best colour to cover it.' Sue shrugs. 'Bit of warmth. It's taken ten years off her – apart from the burns, of course.'

'Oh dear,' Grandad says. 'Well, as I said, Rose has been feeling a bit run down . . .'

Sue looks at him, her eyes full of pity.

'Patrick, I know,' she says. 'It's OK. I just wanted to say – well, tell Rose to take as much time off as she needs. I know she didn't mean it, but I can't afford mistakes like that. Karen and I can cover for her till she's back on track. OK?'

Sue stands up, smoothing down her jeans.

'I – ah – found this at the back of the shampoo cupboard,' she says quietly to Grandad, passing him a bottle-shaped package swathed in carrier bags. 'I thought it best to let you know.'

Grandad has the bottle out of her hands and hidden in the sideboard drawer in less time than it takes to blink.

'Yes, well, lovely to see you again, Sue,' he says quickly, ushering her to the door. 'Don't be a stranger, now. I'll be sure to tell Rose how understanding you've been about . . . well, everything.'

'As I said, Patrick,' Sue says, beaming, 'not a problem.'

Not a problem?

My mum only dyed Miss Devlin's hair green. It could have been anyone, but it had to be Miss Devlin, didn't it? She knows Mum, from Parents' Night. And now she knows that I am the daughter of a mad, hair-dye-wielding maniac. Or, worse . . .

Did she smell the drink on Mum as she painted on the deadly dye-paste? Did she guess? Will she look at me with sad, pitying eyes when I trudge in to registration tomorrow?

I hope not.

Grandad turns the TV on to *Family Fortunes*. Gran's eyes light up as she watches the screen, needles flying, and Toto very daintily leans over and snaffles the jammie dodgers from Sue's untouched plate.

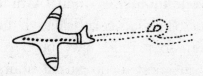

I wake up early, in a cold sweat, after a vivid nightmare in which Mr McGrath, Father Lynch and Miss Devlin (with glowing lime-green hair) chase me off school property, pelting me with bottles of ginger beer, jammie dodgers and snowballs that turn out to be gobbets of hair dye.

Nice. I shower quickly and get dressed, making sure my shirt is crisply ironed, my sweater clean, tie straight. I spend a few minutes polishing my boots to a high shine, on the off chance that perfect school uniform will shield me from the fallout that Miss Devlin's hair disaster is bound to create.

By the time I hear the creak of the stairs, the table is laid for breakfast and I've poured tea for Gran and Grandad.

'That's grand, pet,' Grandad says, huddling into his dressing gown and warming his hands above the toaster. 'You're a good girl, Jude.'

Gran wanders into the kitchen in tartan

slippers and an ankle-length nightdress. Her blue eyes are pale and watery from sleep. She flops into a chair, picking up a bundle of knitting from the fruit bowl.

'No sign of your mum, yet, then?' Grandad sighs, dishing out bowls of cornflakes. 'I didn't hear her come in, so it must have been really late. What does she find to do till all hours of the night?'

'Drink,' I say, coldly. 'That's what she does. Even though she knows what it does to her. It's pathetic!'

'Now, now, Jude,' Grandad says. 'It's an illness, you know. She can't help it.'

'Can't she?' I ask. 'I bet she could help it if she tried. She just doesn't want to. She'd choose whisky over us any day, Grandad, you know she would. She doesn't care how much it hurts us.'

'Who's hurt?' Gran asks, clutching her knitting. 'What's wrong?'

'Nothing's wrong, Molly,' Grandad says softly, putting an arm round her. 'Eat up your cornflakes, now. Jude didn't mean anything.'

'No, of course not,' I whisper. 'It's OK, Gran.'

But Gran is standing now, clutching the mess of yarn to her, eyes wild. 'Something's wrong!' she cries. 'Where's my Rose? What's happened to my Rose?'

Grandad rolls his eyes, coaxes Gran back on to her chair. 'Nothing's happened to Rose,' he says patiently. 'She's upstairs, asleep in bed. Jude's just going to take her a nice cup of coffee.'

'I don't want . . .' I begin, but Grandad gives me a stern look.

'She didn't mean those things she said yesterday,' he tells me. 'She won't even remember them, Jude. It was the drink talking. Take her a coffee and clear the air.'

'She dyed Miss Devlin's hair green,' I say. 'I'll never forgive her.'

'Jude!'

So I shrug and huff and spoon instant coffee into Mum's *drama queen* mug.

I hesitate outside Mum's door and knock, but there's no reply so I push the door open. I expect to see a messy, darkened room stinking of whisky and fags, a rumpled duvet, Mum asleep with a ginger-beer bottle in her arms. Instead, the curtains are wide open, and the dull February light filters in. I can see right away she's not there. The duvet is neat and tidy, the pillow plumped. It's like nobody slept there at all.

My heart starts to race. I look around for Mum's pink leather jacket with the stained cuff, her red stilettos, her handbag. They're missing. She hasn't been home.

'Grandad!' I roar. 'Grandad! Quick!'

He thunders up the stairs, puffs into the doorway behind me.

'Ah, no,' he says. 'Where is she?'

'She's been out all night,' I say, my voice shaking. 'She could be anywhere! Anything could have happened!'

Images of dark alleys, sleazy pubs and strangers crowd into my head, and I push them away again.

'No, no,' Grandad blusters. 'There's no need to worry. She'll be at Sue's or Giovanni's, or one of her new friends' places. Perhaps she couldn't get a taxi.'

'But she always comes home,' I say shakily. 'Always.'

'Of course she does.' Grandad frowns. 'Of course. But perhaps she had just a little bit too much to drink and forgot the time, lost her keys, spent her taxi money . . .'

I blink back tears, thinking of Mum lost and alone in the middle of the night. What if she's had an accident? Or made herself really, really ill, like last time, when it took an ambulance, a bunch of doctors and a long stay in hospital to put things right?

'Don't be upsetting yourself, Jude,' Grandad says firmly. 'It's nothing to worry about, I'm sure.

You go on to school and leave this to me – I'll do some ringing round. By the time you get home, your mum will be back, safe and sound, you'll see.'

'Promise?' I ask, the way I used to when I was little and I thought that Grandad could do anything.

'Promise,' Grandad says. He stretches out a hand to ruffle my hair. 'It'll be all right. Go on to school, Jude – and don't worry.'

I clatter down the stairs, grab my rucksack, blow Gran a kiss. Her knitting yarn is trailing through the dregs of milk and cornflakes on the table, but I pretend not to notice. She looks at me, faintly puzzled, and I know she's struggling to remember who I am.

'I had a daughter, once,' she tells me.

'That's right,' I agree, tucking a strand of grey hair behind her ear. 'I had a mum once too.'

Miss Devlin stalks through the school in her usual no-nonsense manner, with an armful of books and a long, crinkly scarf trailing behind her. She looks amazing. The straggly, mouse-grey layers have gone, replaced by an ash-blonde bob with golden streaks. She has ditched her usual dark trouser suit for a cute flowery skirt and a pale blue fluffy jumper. Fluffy? Miss Devlin?

Mr McGrath stops in his tracks and does a double take as she sweeps past. Then he sees me staring, and goes slightly pink.

In registration, there is a similar reaction. The kids look once, look again, then gawp openly. 'Like the hair, Miss,' Brendan Coyle says, eyes wide.

'Thank you, Brendan.'

'It's too young for her,' Kristina Kowalski whispers nastily, but Miss Devlin doesn't seem to hear. She just smiles to herself and raises one eyebrow, and Brendan tells Kristina to shut up.

Well, at least Miss Devlin isn't mad at me. Nobody has pelted me with ginger-beer bottles, jammie dodgers or hair-dye bombs. Nothing has been said about detentions or lines. I have not been summoned to see Mr McGrath to be expelled, or Father Lynch to confess all my sins. Yet.

Just when I think I've got away with it, Miss Devlin collars me as we trail out of the classroom ready for our first lesson.

'Can I see you for a minute, Jude?' she asks.

'I don't want to be late for history,' I bluster.

'I won't keep you long. It's just – well, I thought we should have a little chat.'

My heart sinks. 'Miss?'

'Jude . . .' she says, kindly. 'Is everything all right at home?'

A blush seeps up from my neck, staining my face with pink. I can't meet her eye. Miss Devlin is brisk, businesslike, strict. I don't think I can cope with kindness, not from her.

'Everything's fine, Miss,' I lie.

'Oh? Well, that's good. But if there were any problems . . . if you ever needed to talk . . .'

My gaze slides past Miss Devlin. I'm looking out of the window, off into the distance where a plane is slicing its way through the vast, blue sky, trailing a long streak of feathery white behind it. I wish I was on that plane, heading for somewhere warm and sunny, leaving my troubles behind. Of course, knowing my luck, I'd be sandwiched in between Gran and Grandad, with Mum across the aisle glugging down the duty-free.

'No problems, Miss,' I say. 'Honestly.'

'Well, if you do need to talk,' Miss Devlin says, 'you know where to find me. It'll all work out in time, Jude, I'm sure.'

I bolt out of there like my tail's on fire. *It'll all work out in time?* Yeah, sure.

My mum could be curled up in an alleyway, mugged, bleeding. She could be stuck in Casualty with a broken ankle, trying to remember her name and address. She could be waking up in some seedy flat with a stranger, rubbing her head and reaching for the next drink.

It's not going to work out, not any time soon.

And Miss Devlin is going to be shooting me sad-eyed looks of pity, probably for the rest of my school career. Great.

I slope along to history and slip into a seat beside Nuala. Mr Jackson's voice drones on endlessly, something about Henry VIII and his six wives. I'm not taking anything in, not even when Carter writes Amber-Lynn up on the whiteboard instead of Anne Boleyn and the class dissolves into giggles.

'What?' Carter demands, baffled. 'It *is* Amber-Lynn, isn't it? What's funny?'

'This is a history lesson, not a soap opera,' Mr Jackson huffs. 'Write me two sides of A4 on Anne Boleyn for homework, Carter. Are you feeling all right, Jude Reilly? You look very pale.'

'I – I don't know,' I say. A whole wave of shudders washes over my body. Even my fingers are shaking.

'She's shivering, Sir,' Nuala says, anxiously.

'Oh dear. Take her along to the office.'

I hide behind my hair and let Nuala lead me from the room.

When you are a bright-eyed, Goody Two-Shoes, high-achieving pupil, nobody expects you to pull a sickie, but hey, I learnt it from my mum. She's an expert.

'How do you feel?' the school nurse asks. 'There's no fever, but you do seem a bit shaky.'

'I feel shaky,' I say, and that's the truth, at least. 'And tired.'

'You may be coming down with something,' the nurse decides. 'Is there anyone in at home? Anyone who can come and pick you up?'

'My gran and grandad are there,' I tell her. 'They haven't got a car, but I could walk. I think the fresh air would help, Miss. It's not far.'

'I'll just ring and make sure they're in.' The nurse purses her lips, taps out the number and speaks briefly to Grandad. 'They're waiting for you,' she says. 'Walk straight home, mind, then stay in the warm with lots of hot drinks. Call the doctor if things seem any worse.'

And that's that. I walk out of school, my rucksack swinging, up the avenue and out along the main road towards Tile Hill. As I pass my old primary school and the church of Our Lady of Sorrows, I can feel the tears prickling my eyes. I'd like to go inside, where it will be dark and safe and quiet, with the smell of incense and candles and wood polish. I'd like to kneel down and close my eyes and pray.

I'd ask for Mum to come home safely, obviously. She'd come home full of regret and apologies, kick the whisky and stop trampling all over my heart in her red stilettos. I'd pray for a nationwide ban on alcohol and Rollerblades too, a dad who doesn't wear rhinestone-studded catsuits and a pass with Merit in my Grade Four piano exam. I don't want tragedy or embarrassment or drama, I just want ordinary. Is that too much to ask?

I get as far as the top of the church steps, but the sound of singing wafts out to me, distant, other-worldly. The kids from the primary school are having a Mass, playing hymns on recorder and guitar and reading chunks of Gospel in halting, sing-song voices.

I duck along the side of the church, round to the back where the little shrine of Our Lady of Sorrows is. This is the place where miracles happen, after all. Some chance.

I fling my rucksack down and slump on to one of the benches, but when I look up at the statue my eyes open wide. There is a boy on the other side of the handrail, sitting at the feet of Our Lady of Sorrows. He is older than me, maybe sixteen, with long tawny-fair hair, pink cheeks and very blue eyes.

The boy is holding half a loaf of uncut white bread, which he is tearing into pieces, scattering on to the rocks nearby like bits of torn tissue. All around him, birds are sitting, sparrows, blackbirds, thrushes, even a robin, pecking at the crumbs of bread. They are so close he could easily reach out his hand and touch half a dozen of them. As I stare, hardly daring to breathe, a couple flutter closer still. One perches on the shoulder of his beige duffel coat, another lands on his denim-patched knee, ruffling its feathers.

The boy holds out a hand, filled with breadcrumbs, and the little brown bird hops right on to his palm. It's the weirdest thing I've ever seen. A sense of magic hangs in the air like mist.

When I was little, Nuala and I sat telling jokes to the statue of Our Lady until our eyes blurred and we thought we saw her smile, but it wasn't a miracle, not really, just wishful thinking.

This is different. The boy with the bread looks spookily like a picture I once saw of a saint called

Francis of Assisi, an Italian monk who lived in a forest surrounded by animals and birds.

Then he speaks, and the illusion fades.

'Wann some?' he asks, looking up, grinning. 'I got lots!'

He has to be at least sixteen, but it's like talking to a little kid. Those amazing blue eyes are clear and bright and sparkly, but there's nothing behind them.

'No thanks, it's OK,' I tell him. 'You have it.'

'Birds,' he says, still grinning.

'Yeah, that's right,' I say gently. 'Birds.'

He's what the teachers call Special Needs, I can see that. Not like Jim at school, who is deaf, or Pete, who has ADHD, or even Cassi, who has some kind of syndrome and has to have a Learning Support teacher with her all the time. They all fit in, no hassle, but I can't imagine this boy in a classroom.

'What's your name?' I ask, but the boy has retreated into a world of his own, pulling the last crumbs from the hollowed-out loaf.

My eyes flick up to the statue of Our Lady of Sorrows. I must be crazy to think she could help look after Mum, bring her home safe, stop her from drinking. Still, old habits die hard.

Please, please, please, I pray. *Please let Mum come home safe. Don't let her get really ill, like last time. Look after Gran and Gramps, help me pass my piano exam and . . . look after the Bird Boy.*

'See you, then,' I call, but the boy doesn't even look up. He's whispering to the robin on his shoulder, a soft stream of nonsense falling from his lips. I can't work out if he's a miracle or a tragedy.

All the way home, I tell myself that Mum will be there, safe and well, cuddled up on the settee with Toto, drinking coffee and watching *The Wizard of Oz*.

When I turn into the street I see Grandad at the gate, scanning the street anxiously. 'There you are,' he says as I approach, taking my school bag and holding a palm against my forehead to check for fever. 'What's wrong, Jude? The school nurse said you were ill.'

'Not really,' I admit. 'She thinks I'm sickening for something, but actually I'm just fed up and worried about Mum. She's still not home, is she?'

'No,' Grandad admits. 'I've called the hospital, and she's not there. Sue hasn't seen her, and there was nobody home at Giovanni's. I suppose he'll be working – doesn't he wash dishes at that Italian restaurant in the winter?'

'She won't be with him, anyway,' I say. 'She doesn't have time for Sue or Giovanni when she's drinking. They worry too much, tell her things she doesn't want to hear.'

'Well,' Grandad says, chewing his lip. 'She's got to be somewhere.'

Gran looks up from her armchair, smiling over her knitting.

'Do you know, I'd love an ice-cream cornet,' she says. 'With a chocolate flake and raspberry sauce.'

'Molly, love, it's February,' Grandad says.

'I know,' Gran says. 'Scorching hot weather too. Should I have nuts as well as raspberry sauce?'

'I suppose I could get some ice cream from the corner shop,' I'm saying, but just then an ice-cream van jingle fills the air. I give Gran a puzzled look, but she just grins back, smug.

'Giovanni!' Grandad exclaims. 'That lad doesn't give up!'

We crowd together at the window. 'Mum!' I squeal. 'She's OK! Giovanni's brought her home!'

Giovanni and Mum walk down the garden path. Mum looks chirpy, happy, but Giovanni is serious. Grandad whips the door open before he can ring the bell.

'Rose, love!' he beams. 'We've been so worried!'

'It was all a misunderstanding,' Mum says. 'Ridiculous.'

Giovanni shakes his head. I've never seen him look angry before, but he does today.

'What happened?' I want to know. 'Where were you?'

Mum just shrugs off her pink leather jacket, flinging it down on to a chair.

'Come on,' Giovanni says, coldly. 'Tell her, Rosa. Tell your daughter where you spent the night.'

'It was a load of rubbish!' Mum bursts out. 'I tried to tell them, but they wouldn't listen. Idiots!'

'Who?' Grandad asks, but Mum just flops down on to the settee, picks up the remote control and clicks the TV on. Giovanni leans down, unsmiling, and takes the remote control away, switching the TV off. Mum unleashes a torrent of abuse, finally taking off a red stiletto to hurl at Giovanni. It misses and lands rakishly in Gran's knitting bag.

'Oh dear,' she says, mildly.

'She called me an hour ago because she didn't want you to know,' Giovanni says calmly. 'She asked me to pick her up – from the police station. She spent the night in the cells!'

Mum launches herself at Giovanni, swearing, screaming, punching, scratching. Giovanni just peels her off, like she's a toddler with a tantrum. She sinks back on to the settee, crying.

'It was a mistake, all right?' she says between sobs. 'I wasn't doing anything wrong! I was just tired, that's all, and I sat down for a little rest . . .'

'Students found her in the city centre,' Giovanni

tells us. 'Collapsed in the gutter. They thought she was ill and called 999, but of course, she was only drunk. When the police tried to talk to her to find out where she lived, she screamed and swore at them. They took her in for a night in the cells. She was lucky not to be charged with Drunk and Disorderly.'

I am frozen with shame and horror. A dark flush creeps over my cheeks, and I can't think of a single thing to say.

'Oh, Rose, no,' Grandad whispers.

'I didn't mean it!' she protests. 'OK, I'd had a bit too much to drink, but that's not a crime, is it? Is it? I was just tired!'

I have sick visions of classmates, teachers, neighbours, all wandering past, frowning and asking themselves if the drunk in the gutter didn't look just like Jude Reilly's mum. I know I should feel concerned, anxious, upset, but all I can feel is embarrassed, angry.

'Anything could have happened, Rose!' Grandad says sadly. 'Thank God those students found you. You could have frozen to death!'

'As if you'd care!' Mum snaps. 'A night in the cells is no picnic, either, let me tell you! There were all kinds of nasty types in there. Imagine locking up a poor, defenceless woman . . .' She wraps her arms around herself, like a little girl snuggling up in the cold, shutting out the world. 'I didn't mean it,' she says.

'Of course not, love,' Grandad soothes. He fusses around her, picking up a blue fleece blanket to tuck round her shoulders, like Gran used to do for me when I was little and feeling sad. 'Don't worry, Rose, pet. You're home now, safe and sound. It's all over.'

I wish I could believe that. Mum says she's tired and upset and needs to lie down. She slopes away up the stairs, while Grandad shakes Giovanni's hand and tells him he's a grand fellow.

'You've always been there for Rose,' he says. 'We appreciate that. Stay for a nice cup of tea, now. We've got wafer biscuits, a new packet.'

He bustles out to the kitchen, and Giovanni turns to me.

'I can't do it,' he says, the minute Grandad is out of earshot. 'I can't stand by and watch her do this, you know?'

'We don't have much of a choice, do we?' I say, and then I realize that Giovanni actually does. We're family, but he's not. Why should he hang around to be treated like dirt?

'I can't go on pretending it doesn't matter,' Giovanni says. 'It does. Today, when I collected her from the station – it was horrible, Jude. I was ashamed.'

I know, because I'm ashamed too.

'Then, in the van, she told me she didn't want to go back home – didn't want to face you. Never mind that you'd all be out of your minds with worry. We're driving along, me going on about detox clinics and Alcoholics Anonymous, and Rosa just smiles sweetly and asks me to take her to a bar. A bar, Jude! After all that! Can you believe it?'

A tear leaks out from the corner of my eye and slides down my cheek, and my stomach feels cold, sour, empty.

'I can't do this,' Giovanni declares. 'Unless she can admit she has a problem, unless she can ask for some help to get herself well again . . . and she cannot. She will not. It is over for me, Jude. Over.'

'Not really,' I say, uncertainly. 'I mean, you'll be around, won't you? When she gets better. It's not really the *end* or anything, is it?'

But Giovanni just looks at me, all sad brown eyes and slanting brows, and my heart sinks.

'I can't do it, Jude,' he says. 'I can't just watch her drink herself to death.'

Gran, Grandad and I don't have that choice, of course.

'I am sorry,' Giovanni says.

I'm sorry too. Giovanni has been a part of our lives for almost three years now. He is sweet and funny and kind, but Mum has always treated him badly, even when she's not drinking. When she's sober, she lets him take her on dates and days out, buy her flowers, chocolates. He's not Mr Perfect, she says, but he'll do for now.

'He loves me, Jude,' she told me, once. 'That has to count for something, doesn't it?'

Apparently not. Giovanni tells me to explain to Grandad that he is heartbroken, that the tea would only choke him. He slips out of the front door, walks down the path, shoulders drooping.

'Over,' Gran echoes sadly, still cradling Mum's scuffed red stiletto.

I remember the ice-cream cornet then, and run down the path after Giovanni to ask him.

'For Molly, anything,' he says, smiling sadly. He hands me a huge cornet, complete with chocolate flake, raspberry sauce and nut sprinkles, and tells me to look after myself. I stand on the path and watch as the ice-cream van pulls away from the kerb, chugs along the road and disappears round the corner.

Tears sting my eyes, but I sniff them back and walk inside, holding the ice-cream cornet.

'There you are, Gran,' I whisper, forcing a smile. 'For you.'

She looks at me as though I'm crazy. 'Ice cream?' she says. 'Oh, no, Jude, not for me. I couldn't – brrr! Don't you know it's only February?'

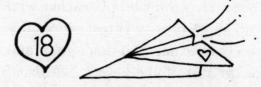

'So,' says Carter, slipping into the seat beside me. He's finally joined Brendan Coyle's street hockey team, and he has a spectacular black eye to show for it. 'No Nuala today?'

'Well spotted,' I say.

Nuala is at the orthodontist. It's art, and I am looking forward to a quiet afternoon of still-life drawing. Instead I get Carter. Lucky me.

Mr Latimer is telling us about chalk and charcoal, about looking for shape and pattern and tone and texture. I look at the heap of rusting bicycle wheels arranged on the table in front of me, but no matter how hard I try, they're just a heap of rusting bicycle wheels.

'Great viewpoint from here,' Carter says. 'You don't mind if I sit in Nuala's seat this lesson, do you?'

'I'm overjoyed,' I say, flatly.

'Thought so!'

Mr Latimer puts Radio One on and sits down

with the newspaper crossword and a mug of coffee. He's the kind of teacher who baffles you with long words and great expectations, then rolls his eyes because you don't get it and blanks you for the rest of the lesson. Not that I care – not today, anyhow. I pick up a piece of chalk and make a couple of half-hearted marks.

'Anyway,' Carter says, 'I was hoping I'd get a chance to talk to you. I was wondering if you fancied coming to the skate park one night?'

'I'd rather eat my own shoe,' I reply.

'Uh?' Carter frowns at my footwear, looking for possible clues. 'Does that mean . . . no?'

'It means no.'

Carter looks floored, as though this is one possibility he hasn't considered. 'OK, no. Maybe skating's not your thing.'

'Carter, skating's not *your* thing, either,' I point out. 'You're hopeless.'

'I'm getting better!'

'No, you're not. Why don't you just admit it and give up?'

He grins at me from behind the floppy, straw-coloured hair. 'I'm not the giving-up kind, Jude,' he tells me. 'Haven't you noticed?'

'Yeah, I've noticed.'

'It's called determination,' Carter says.

'It's called stupidity,' I correct him.

'I love it when you're mad at me,' he says. 'But you're wrong. I'm not stupid.'

I raise an eyebrow and shake my head.

'It's not stupid to hope, is it?' Carter asks.

Oh boy. Yes it is, seriously stupid, dangerously stupid. You hope and dream and nothing ever changes. People let you down, stuff goes pear-shaped. I know this from long experience. And I am never, ever going to go out with Kevin Carter. As if.

Kristina Kowalski wiggles across the room, tottering on black stiletto boots that look like the toes have been finished off in Mr Latimer's industrial pencil sharpener. She sees Carter beside me and frowns.

'What you sitting with *her* for, Kevin?' she wants to know. 'Come and sit with me and Brendan!'

'Nah, I'm OK, thanks.' Carter shrugs.

'What, is she doing your maths homework for you or something?'

'Go away, Kristina,' Carter says.

'Touchy! I was only asking! I mean, she's not exactly your type, is she?' Kristina smirks. 'Not anybody's type, really!'

Carter just stares her out, but I let my long hair slide forward, hide behind it, blushing. I hate Kristina Kowalski, I really do.

'Maybe I'm wrong,' she says, finally. 'Maybe you're a good match. Two losers. Hey, Brendan, guess what? Carter's got the hots for Jude Reilly!'

She tosses her long tawny hair over her shoulder, as if to show Carter what he's missing, then flounces off to where Brendan and his cronies are sitting, laughing and wolf-whistling in our direction.

Great.

'She's jealous,' Carter tells me. 'Obvious, isn't it?'

'Er, I don't think so!' But Carter just grins to himself, savouring the wolf whistles until they die down and Brendan goes back to his work. Luckily for us, art is his favourite subject.

'Why did you join his stupid street hockey team, anyway?' I ask, steering the conversation on to safer ground. 'You're useless, and you know it. Brendan only wants you in the team so he can beat you up with a clear conscience.'

'It's a tough game, but I can take it,' Carter says, heroically.

'I can see that,' I reply. 'I suppose that black eye didn't hurt?'

'It's not really black, more purplish,' Carter says. 'With mottled green and yellow bits around the edges. Those hockey sticks can be lethal.'

'Especially when you're around. Face it, Carter, you're just not coordinated.'

'Rubbish!' he protests, hoisting his grey combats up a few inches to reveal matching Simpsons socks. 'See?'

'Not that kind of coordinated! Seriously, Carter, pack it in before you wind up in hospital!'

Mr Latimer is doing a lazy circuit of the room, sipping his coffee and peering at the work. I pick up the charcoal and make a few hasty circle shapes, then some random straight lines to represent the spokes.

'Nice,' Mr Latimer comments, taking a look. 'Very abstract.' He tells Carter that his sketch looks like a plate of spaghetti Bolognese.

'He likes it really,' Carter grins. 'So. If I was in hospital, would you visit? You could feed me grapes and chocolates.'

'In your dreams,' I say.

'Yeah, in my dreams. Not the skate park, then – how about a meal out?'

'Don't tell me – the hospital canteen?'

Carter looks hurt. 'I was thinking of the chippy,' he says. 'They do deep-fried Mars bars, you know. What are you doing after school?'

'Piano lesson.'

'Another one?' Carter looks horrified. 'Nah. Are you sure you're not meeting some sixth-former with a leather jacket and a motorbike?'

'I have a piano exam coming up, I told you,'

I huff. 'I need to practise. Look, Carter, this conversation is going nowhere. Forget it.'

'You're not talking to me?'

I add a few areas of random tone and texture to my drawing, pretending to be fascinated by the rusty bike wheels.

'Seriously?' Carter demands. 'You're blanking me? No way! Jude? Speak to me, please! We were planning our first date. You can't just leave it there!'

I use a corner of my tissue to do some careful smudging, then blow off the chalk dust and call it a day.

'Jude?'

I'm just flicking through my music theory notebook when a tiny paper plane lands in my lap. I brush it off on to the floor, but within seconds it's back again. It makes a series of unplanned landings, on my drawing, in my rucksack, on my music theory book.

'Open it,' Carter hisses. 'It's really important.'

I open it out carefully, smoothing the creases, to see the message inside. *Do you prefer mushy peas or curry sauce?* it says. I try to keep my face grim and forbidding, but a bubble of laughter escapes from my mouth before I can stop it. Carter is looking at me, grinning. I try to hide behind my hand, but more giggles leak out until I'm laughing and laughing. Every time I try to stop, I catch Carter's eye and we fall apart all over again, until my eyes are damp with tears and my lips ache from grinning.

'Look at the lovebirds,' Kristina Kowalski calls over. 'What's the joke, you two? Oh sorry, I forgot. *You* are!'

'Definitely jealous,' Carter says.

'No, definitely curry sauce.'

Later, when the bell has gone and we've packed up and everyone is heading for the door in a big messy scrum, Carter leans over, scarily close.

'I won't give up,' he whispers, and this time I smile.

Mum has been different all week. She isn't going out, she isn't acting mean, and she doesn't seem to be drinking or smoking as much. A couple of times before, she's pulled herself back from the edge, cleaned up her act, got sober. Giovanni was the one who helped her then, driving her to AA meetings and talking her through the bad times, whatever the time of day or night.

'You can do it,' he used to tell her. 'Do it for me.'

Right now, though, he's not picking up her calls, not answering her messages. She knows he's mad at her, but she doesn't realize she's been dumped. I'm not going to be the one to tell her.

On Thursday, when I come downstairs, Mum's already in the kitchen. She looks neat and chirpy, her hair still damp from the shower.

'OK, Jude?' she says, and you could almost kid yourself she was a normal mum. She sets two plates of scrambled eggs down on the table, pours out orange juice.

'What's the occasion?' I ask.

'No occasion,' she says. 'Do I need an excuse to have breakfast with my lovely daughter?'

'Suppose not,' I grin. 'Thanks, Mum!' I scoop up a forkful of buttery eggs and take a bite of toast. 'I could get used to this!'

'I'm not a bad cook, when I try,' Mum admits. 'Maybe I should open a cafe? Or write cookery books! Not the fancy kind, just good, basic recipes for good, ordinary families!'

'Great.' I nod, although I'm pretty sure that what Mum knows about good, ordinary families would fit on the back of a postage stamp. 'Go for it, Mum. You're looking much better. Happier. Not so . . . well, you know.'

Mum frowns and sips her orange juice. 'I'm going to get healthy,' she tells me. 'I've probably been overdoing it a bit lately, but that . . . that *misunderstanding* in town really made me see sense. I made you a promise, didn't I Jude? I haven't forgotten. I won't let you down.'

Hope rises inside me again, and I find myself believing that, somehow, things can still be OK. Maybe.

Miss Lloyd, my piano teacher, receives a letter telling her that my Grade Four piano exam has been scheduled for 5.10 p.m. on Friday 31 March.

'You're ready,' she tells me. 'Your pieces are beautiful, and you know your scales, arpeggios and broken chords. Just stay calm on the day and you'll do well.'

'I can't!' I protest. 'I won't be here. I'll be in Gretna Green, for my dad's wedding!'

'He's getting married on 31 March?' Miss Lloyd frowns.

'Well, no, the wedding is the next morning,' I admit. 'But I'm driving up to Scotland on the Friday, with Dad and Victoria.'

'Oh dear,' Miss Lloyd says. 'These things can be difficult to rearrange, and you've worked so hard! Is there no other way?'

I play a couple of scales, trying to get my head straight.

'I could go by train,' I say, uncertainly. 'Dad and Victoria could meet me at the station.'

'Do you think so, dear?' Miss Lloyd asks. 'Do you want me to give them a call and explain what's happened?'

She does, and after my lesson I walk round to the house to see them. Dad and Victoria are upset I can't travel up to Scotland with them in the pink Cadillac, but they agree I can't miss my piano exam.

'I wish we hadn't arranged the Elvis karaoke for Friday night,' Dad huffs. 'It's a kind of pre-wedding party, instead of a stag and hen do. Just about everyone's said they'll be there – people have booked their hotel rooms already. We can't really change it now.'

'Of course you can't,' I tell him. 'It's your special night! It's OK. I'll get the train.'

'Maybe Andy and Lori could give you a lift on Saturday?' he muses. 'No, they're already bringing Jeff, Jane and Lindsey. Everyone else is coming the day before, or else coming from different places.'

'The train will be fine,' I say.

Victoria makes some phone calls and orders me a return ticket for the 18.23 train. I have to change at Birmingham and Carlisle to arrive in Gretna some time after eleven. Victoria has reserved a seat for me in the Quiet Carriage on the main Carlisle train.

'It's very late for a thirteen-year-old to be out by herself,' she says. 'Train stations can be funny places. Let's forget the change at Carlisle – I'll slip away from the karaoke and meet you at Carlisle.'

'Good idea,' Dad says. 'We both will. How's that?'

I don't want to drag Dad and Victoria away from their party, but being met at Carlisle sounds way better than wandering around a strange railway station at night, trying to find my connecting train.

'Thanks.' I grin. 'That'd be brilliant.'

'So that's only one change you have to manage,' Victoria says. 'The trouble is, Birmingham is such a big, busy station. I wonder . . .'

'I'll give your grandad a quick ring,' Dad says, and five minutes later it's all arranged; Grandad will come on the train with me to Birmingham, see me on to the connecting train, and then travel back to Coventry.

'Honestly, I'm not a kid,' I tell them. 'I could easily manage.' But secretly, I'm glad I don't have to. Victoria picks up the phone again and orders a return ticket to Birmingham for Grandad.

'There,' says Dad. 'Sorted! And you still get to travel in the pink Cadillac!'

I catch Victoria's eye and pull a face, making sure Dad can't see.

'Lucky me,' I say.

Giovanni still isn't answering Mum's calls.

'I'm worried about him,' she says. 'Perhaps he's lost his phone, or broken it or something? I've left him lots of messages, but now when I call, it just says the number is unobtainable.'

I shrug. Maybe he's lost his phone, maybe he's leaving it switched off, or maybe he's just blacklisted Mum's number so his mobile won't accept her calls?

We're at the kitchen table, Mum sipping black coffee and painting her nails, me struggling through history homework. Gran, Grandad and Toto are huddled in the living room, watching some prehistoric black-and-white film.

'I just want to tell him how grateful I am for everything he did the other day,' Mum is saying. 'It gave me a real scare, Jude. It was the most humiliating, horrible experience. The more I tried to tell them they were making a mistake, the worse it got. You can't imagine it, really you can't.'

135

I can. Really, I can.

'And Giovanni rescued me,' Mum goes on. 'I was tired and upset and angry, and perhaps I wasn't as grateful as I should have been . . .'

'You threw a shoe at him,' I point out.

'Did I?' Mum asks. 'Well, he can be such a nag, always telling me what to do, how to live my life. But I know all that is because he loves me, Jude. It's because he cares.'

'Right,' I say carefully, keeping my head bent low over my homework. I bet Queen Elizabeth I didn't have all this trouble with her family. Of course, they were all dead or locked up in the Tower of London, so perhaps that's why.

'So I like a drink,' Mum says, sadly. 'So do lots of people. What's wrong with that?'

'It's not good to overdo it,' I say carefully.

'No, of course not,' Mum agrees. 'And I have been overdoing it, I know. That's not a good thing, I can see that. I know you've all been worried about me, but there's no need – I've got my act together now, haven't I? I'm making a fresh start, I promise. No more late nights, no more ciggies, no more drink.'

I look up, eyes wide.

'You're giving up? Completely?' I ask, heart thumping.

'I said so, didn't I? It's not like I have a *problem*,

not really. I just like the stuff, that's all! I can give it up if I want to.'

'You could go to those AA meetings for help and support,' I suggest. 'You said that helped, last time.'

Mum shakes her head. 'I just said that to please Giovanni,' she explains. 'AA meetings aren't for me. I mean – Alcoholics Anonymous – well, I'm not an alcoholic, am I?'

I can't meet her eyes. 'I don't know,' I whisper.

'Oh, Jude, of *course* I'm not,' Mum laughs, and the way she says it I almost believe her. 'I decided to give up and I've done it. I don't need doctors or counsellors or anyone else to tell me what to do – I'm doing it for me. Me and you, Jude.'

I'm grinning all over my face, and my eyes mist with tears. What does it matter which label you stick on a problem? It's fixing it that counts. It's going to be all right, I know it is.

'I've changed, Jude,' Mum tells me. 'I'm going to be a better mum, truly. And I want Giovanni to know that I've changed. I've listened to his advice, taken control of my life. I just want him to *know* that. I want him to be proud of me.'

'He will be,' I argue. I hope that's true.

Mum grins, draining her coffee. 'So, come on!' she tells me. 'Let's go and tell him! He works evenings at the restaurant, but I bet he could take a night off to take his two favourite girls out for a pizza! Come *on*!'

We're laughing like a couple of kids, grabbing our coats, shouting goodbye to Gran and Grandad, tumbling out on to the pavement. Mum links my arm and strides along, so fast I'm half running, trying to keep up. 'He's OK, Giovanni,' she tells me. 'He doesn't have much of a head for business, but he's kind. Sometimes, Jude, all you want in life is someone who's there for you, someone who cares.'

'I care,' I reply.

'Of course you do,' Mum laughs. 'I know that. Your gran and grandad care too. But that's because you have to, isn't it? You're my daughter, they're my parents. You're *supposed* to care.'

I don't love my mum because I'm 'supposed' to, I love her because she's crazy and quirky and caring and fun, and that somehow balances out the bad stuff. I love her because I can't help it, she's a part of me, and she always will be. I try to tell her this, but she's not listening.

'Boyfriends are different,' she tells me. 'You'll understand when you're older. They look at you and they see something special, and even though they don't know you, not really, they want to. That kind of love is special. It's like an unexpected gift, a parcel left on the doorstep in the middle of the night when it's not your birthday or Christmas or anything.'

I think about Carter, and I smile into the darkness.

'Of course,' Mum is saying, 'it's not always forever. Sometimes, men let you down. Your dad did, and Tom did. Giovanni, though, he's different. He won't let me down.'

I remember Giovanni's serious face, the things he said the day he dropped Mum home from the police station. A needle of doubt pierces my happiness.

'We'd be a good team, Giovanni and I,' Mum rushes on. 'He's wasted with that silly ice-cream van, and I'm not going to throw my life away doing shampoo-and-sets for little old ladies in Sue's dreary old salon. No, Giovanni and I could go into business together – open an Italian ice-cream parlour!'

This image is so enticing, it chases away my anxieties. 'I could make Banana Splits!' I suggest.

'And Knickerbocker Glories,' Mum adds. 'We'd have decadent ice-cream sundaes in tall, cut-glass dishes and low-fat frozen yoghurts piled high with fresh fruit . . . Oh, it could be the new trend! They have chains of coffee shops, soup bars, juice bars . . . why not this?'

'Why not?'

We're still laughing when we burst in through the front door of Mario's Italian restaurant, and our voices seem too loud, too raucous above the soft music. Diners look up at us across the candlelit tables, wondering what the commotion is, and a white-shirted waiter glides towards us quickly, his face disapproving.

'We have no tables free, Madame, I am sorry,' he says, but Mum tells him we're not here to eat, we want to see Giovanni, can we just go through? The waiter says it is not really permitted to speak to staff when they're on duty, but Mum just laughs and strides past him, pulling me along behind.

When we walk through the swing door into the kitchen, things get even frostier. 'What the hell . . . ?' the chef wants to know, but Giovanni rushes forward, full of apologies.

'Five minutes?' he appeals, and the chef nods tightly, his face like thunder. Giovanni herds us through the tiny scullery at the back of the kitchen where he washes the pans and loads the dishwasher, out into a small yard lit only by a pool of light from inside.

'Rosa, what are you doing here?' he demands. 'I'm working! You will get me into trouble!'

'I thought you could take the night off and take us out for a meal,' Mum falters. 'I wanted to thank you for the other day . . .'

'Rosa, no,' he says, exasperated. I can see he is angry, not amused, and I know he hasn't changed his mind about Mum.

'I didn't tell her,' I whisper to him. 'I couldn't.'

'No, Jude, it was wrong of me not to do it,' he says. 'I'll tell her.'

'Tell me what?' Mum demands. 'What's the big secret?'

'I'm sorry it has to be this way, Rosa,' Giovanni says, and Mum's face falls and she starts talking fast, so fast Giovanni can't get a word in edgeways.

'I'm so, so sorry we argued,' she begins. 'I was tired and upset and I really didn't mean those things I said, I didn't, Giovanni, really. I know you only want what's best for me. I've cleaned up my act, I've changed, done everything you asked me to. You tell him, Jude. Tell him!'

'She has,' I say, helplessly. 'Honest.'

'You are going to AA?' he asks, chewing his lip.

'No, not that,' Mum admits. 'Not that, but everything else. I called Sue and she says I can start back next week. I've stopped smoking and I'm not drinking. Seriously, I haven't touched a single drop since that day . . .'

'You've stopped drinking?' Giovanni says. 'Truly, Rosa?'

'Truly,' Mum says. They look at each other so

hard, so long, that even though it's dark out here, I feel like I shouldn't be watching. The moment is too special, too private. Slowly, I see the cold mask drop away from Giovanni's face. He holds out his hands and Mum takes them, and he pulls her close, close enough to kiss.

I wish I was somewhere else, anywhere else, but I'm not, I'm here. I turn my face away.

'No!' Giovanni shouts suddenly, pushing Mum to arm's length. 'No, Rosa, you are not sober. Why do you lie to me?'

Right there in the dark, everything falls to bits, and I know I'll never believe in promises again, because they don't mean anything, not anything at all.

'No, no,' Mum protests. 'I'm not lying! I haven't touched a drop since that day, I swear it!'

'Liar!' he snaps. 'Liar! I can smell it on your breath – and the cigarettes too! D'you think I am stupid?'

'Giovanni, no, it was just a tiny sip, the littlest bit to give me the courage to come and see you!' Mum argues. 'Can't you understand that? Can't you forgive that? OK, so I'm not perfect, but I'm trying, Giovanni, I am!'

He wipes a hand over his eyes, and in the darkness it looks like he's crying, but that could be a trick of the light.

'It's over,' he says, flatly. 'I'm sorry, Rosa.'

Mum pulls her shoulders back, holds her head high.

'Well, maybe it is over, Giovanni,' she agrees. 'Maybe so. But it's over because I say so, you loser. Because *I* say so, OK?'

Then she turns on her heel, grabs up my hand and drags me back through the scullery, the kitchen, the restaurant, everyone staring, mouths open. When she gets to the door, she looks round at all the diners, the couples, the families, and she says she hopes they've all had a good look and she hopes their spaghetti chokes them. Then she drags me out on to the pavement and slams the door so hard behind us that the glass cracks from corner to corner, in little zigzags, like those graphs they make us draw in maths sometimes.

A couple of waiters come out after us and say that they're going to call the police, but Mum just laughs and shouts something so rude I cover my ears, and she grabs my hand and we run and run until we can't run any more.

Carter rings just about every night to ask if I'd like to go out with him, skating or swimming or to the movies. I say no, so he suggests a bike ride, a cross-country run, a trip in a hot-air balloon far, far above the city.

'Do you know how much a trip in a hot-air balloon costs?' I ask him.

'I've got a fiver left over from my Christmas money,' he tells me, proudly.

'Exactly,' I say. 'No chance. Besides, I haven't said I'll go out with you.'

'You will,' Carter says. 'You will.'

'I won't,' I correct him. 'I can't. It's complicated.'

'Should I come round and talk to your grandad?' he asks. 'Would that help?'

'No!' I shriek. 'Seriously, Carter, stay away. It's nothing to do with Grandad – I just don't have time for boyfriends.'

'I'm different,' he says, confidently. 'Make time.'

'Can't,' I say. 'Sorry.'

'Life doesn't have to be complicated,' Carter says.

I look through the doorway into the living room. Grandad is huffing and emptying drawers, pockets and bags out all over the rug, looking for something, and Gran is knitting a long, black scarf and watching *Who Wants To Be a Millionaire?* Mum is asleep on the settee, still in her pyjamas, a bottle of so-called ginger beer stuffed in behind the cushions and Toto at her feet. She's stopped trying to hide it, stopped trying to pretend, ever since that night with Giovanni. I don't know exactly how much she's drinking, but it's a lot. She doesn't care any more.

Complicated? That doesn't even start to cover it.

I say goodbye to Carter and pad through to the kitchen to make tea for Gran and Grandad. 'Lost something?' I ask, lowering the mugs on to the coffee table.

'It was in my wallet, I know it was,' Grandad grunts. 'Either there or in my coat pocket. Where else could it be?'

He leans over and scrabbles about in Gran's knitting bag, and she swats him off with the tail end of the scarf.

'What was?' I ask, scooping everything back

into the emptied drawers and slotting them back into the sideboard while Grandad roots through his wallet and his pockets yet again.

'I must be getting forgetful,' he grumbles, scratching his head. 'I cashed my pension on Monday, and Molly's. I did a food shop, and then I put some aside to pay the phone bill, and now I just can't find it! Forty quid doesn't vanish, just like that!'

'No, it doesn't,' I say grimly, and my eyes slide over to Mum, then back to Grandad. She wouldn't, though. She really, really wouldn't. Would she?

'Really, Patrick, you're getting very forgetful,' Gran sighs, and Grandad's eyes open wide. He hugs her gently, laughing.

'Perhaps I am,' he says, and we leave it at that.

On Thursday afternoon, after school, I call into Thorntons in town to buy my piano teacher a box of chocolates. It's a tradition at exam time.

Tomorrow afternoon I'll go straight from school to Miss Lloyd's. I'll have one final lesson, then the two of us will head into town to the exam hall. Once it's all over, I'll give Miss Lloyd the box of chocolates to thank her for all her help, and Grandad will meet me outside, to walk to the station and catch the 18.23 train.

Dad and Victoria have already got my suitcase, complete with toothbrush, undies and that spectacularly hideous sugar-pink dress. They're taking it up to the hotel tomorrow morning, so I don't have to worry about anything except a drink and a sandwich for the train. It's all arranged.

I pick out a big box of truffles with a gold bow. Grade Four is hard work, and I couldn't have done it without Miss Lloyd. Well, I haven't done it yet, but I will.

'That's £6.75 please,' the assistant says, and I take out my purse, unzip the pocket. The ten pound note I've been saving all week isn't there, and my heart plummets. I unzip the other pocket, but all I find there is a bus pass, a library card, a small photo of me and Mum and Toto. The money's gone.

'Hang on,' I tell the assistant. 'It's definitely here somewhere.' I start a long rummage through my bag, unpacking maths worksheets and exercise books and crumpled gym kit all over the floor of the shop. The assistant moves on to the next customer, leaving me to pull out the pockets of my blazer, pick along the lining of my empty rucksack, my fingers finding crisp crumbs, lost biros, strawberry-flavoured lipgloss, but no tenner.

I repack my bag, pink-faced.

'Sorry,' I tell the assistant. 'I'll have to come back.'

'Perhaps you've spent it already!' she says, cheerily. 'Happens to me all the time!'

It doesn't happen to me, though. I don't have enough money in the first place to get muddled up about what I have and haven't got. I don't go losing whole chunks of it, and nor does Grandad. This has never happened before.

Somebody's taken it, and I just bet I know who.

Mum.

I'm supposed to be home early. I'm supposed to practise my piano stuff for an hour, eat, then practise some more. Dad's going to ring to wish me luck in the exam tomorrow, and make sure everything is ready for afterwards, the train journey north. Carter will probably ring too. Then, Grandad says, I'm to have a long bath, an early night and dream sweet dreams all night long.

Some chance.

I don't want to go home, because it doesn't feel like a home any more, not when your own mum has been going through your purse, taking money to buy drink.

I start walking instead, following the bus route, the way Carter and I walked on the last day of term, in the snow. I wish he was with me now. It's not snowing today, but it's cold, and before long it's dark too, street lamps sparkling orange above me.

When I get to the church of Our Lady of

Sorrows, I turn off the pavement, cut across the car park. I don't believe in miracles any more, but I could use one today.

When I get round to the back of the church, I stop short. In the pool of light around the shrine of Our Lady of Sorrows, I can see the Bird Boy, sitting with his back against the kneeling rail. There are no birds around him tonight – it's dark, after all, and he doesn't seem to have any bread.

He's just sitting, huddled, his legs bunched up in front of him, long light-brown hair hiding his face. He's wearing a handknitted sweater instead of the duffel coat, the kind that doting grannies might knit for a favourite toddler. Its brash primary colours and cartoon motif look all wrong on a teenager.

'Hello,' I say.

He looks up, his blue eyes starred with tears.

'What's wrong?' I ask, forgetting my own troubles in a minute. 'What happened?' I edge closer slowly, not wanting to scare him, but he's not scared of me. He's wrapped up in some sadness of his own. I shrug off my rucksack and sit down next to him. 'What's wrong?' I repeat.

He looks at me then, and holds out his hand for me to see. In his palm, tiny and still and perfect, there is a dead bird. It's green, with a vivid flash of yellow edging its grey wings, a sliver of lime at its tail. A greenfinch, I think.

'Oh no,' I whisper. 'That's sad. Where did you find it?'

Bird Boy doesn't try to answer that. 'Gone,' he sniffs. 'All gone.'

'It's dead,' I tell him, gently. 'Maybe it was just old? Or maybe it flew into a car, or a cat got it.'

We look at the bird, still perfect, its twiggy little legs pink and tipped with claw-like feet, its black eyes still shiny, the downy feathers on its head as soft as silk. We sit in silence for a long time, him cradling the little bird and snuffling quietly. Finally, he wipes his nose on his sleeve, pulls a hand across his eyes to dry the tears, and gives me the dead greenfinch.

I'm horrified.

'Oh, no, really, it's OK,' I falter, giving it back quickly. 'I don't want it!'

'Dead,' Bird Boy says, offering me the bird again. And then I realize what he means, and I jump up, kicking around the stones at my feet until I find a piece of slate that's big enough and long enough to dig with. We squeeze round the side of the handrail, him perched on a rock while I find a patch of dark soil and weeds and dig down, hollowing out a little grave.

Bird Boy lowers the dead bird in, and I pick

some primrose flowers from the little plants tucked in among the rocks and drop the pale-yellow flower heads down on top of the green feathers. I fill in the hole and Bird Boy carefully wedges the piece of slate across the top of it, like a flattened tombstone.

We edge back out and lean against the handrail. 'What's your name?' I ask him. 'Mine's Jude.'

''lo, Jude,' he says.

'What's your name?'

He smiles, and it's like the sun coming out. 'Alex,' he says.

'Hello, Alex. Where do you live?'

'Live there!' He points towards the tall, overgrown hedge that divides the church car park from the houses beyond.

'Nobody lives in a hedge,' I argue, but at that moment a distant voice starts shouting, 'Alex, Alex! Where are you?' Bird Boy must live on the other side of the hedge, in one of the big old houses.

'Not yet,' he says, sulky.

'It's probably teatime,' I explain. 'They'll be worried about you.'

'Alex?' The voice is much nearer now, but Bird Boy isn't answering. 'Alex? Come on! Dad's home. Are you there?'

There's a rustling, crackling noise and a tawny, tousled head appears through a gap in the hedge. I can't believe it. It's Kristina Kowalski, on her hands and knees in the dirt, with twigs in her hair.

'Alex, come on, Dad's looking for you, and it's nearly time to eat . . .' Her voice fizzles out as she catches sight of my shoes, and her eyes travel slowly, disgustedly, upwards until they lock with mine. She gets to her feet, brushing dead leaves from her sprayed-on hipster jeans.

'You!' she splutters in disgust. 'Well, that's just great. What are *you* doing here?'

'Alex!' A new, deeper voice shouts out from behind the hedge. 'Come on, son! It's getting late!'

Alex dives for the gap in the hedge and scrambles through without a backward glance. 'Comin', Dad,' he shouts. 'Comin'!'

I look at Kristina, who is picking a twig from her hair. Same light-brown hair, same blue eyes as Bird Boy. 'Alex is your brother,' I say.

'So?' she snaps. 'So what if he is?'

'You told everyone at school you were an only child.'

'Look, just shut up about this, OK?' Kristina bursts out. 'It's none of your business whether I have a brother or not. Just forget you ever saw me, or Alex. You'd better not go shooting your mouth off about him, Jude Reilly, understand? He has enough problems without losers like you adding to them . . .'

'Why did you say you were an only child?' I repeat, baffled.

Kristina chews her lip. 'Please, Jude,' she says, her voice softer. 'Please don't say anything at school.'

And then it dawns on me – this is the reason Kristina Kowalski is such a mystery girl. This is the reason she doesn't have friends round to the house. She doesn't want anyone to find out about Alex.

'I like Alex,' I say, frowning. 'You can't be . . . *ashamed* of him.'

'I'm not ashamed!' she flings back, fiercely. 'It's not that. It's just . . . look, I've had years of being Alex Kowalski's little sister. At home, Alex comes first – he has to, I understand that, but it's still hard. Outside, it's even worse. Adults feel sorry for him, kids make fun of him, nobody actually sees the person inside. Back in London, I spent the whole time standing up for him, being strong for him, because he couldn't do it for himself.'

Kristina's face is creased and clouded in the dim light from the church wall. She looks like she might cry, or maybe slap my face, I can't tell which.

'Then we moved here,' Kristina tells me. 'We're on the edge of the catchment area for St Joe's, so there's nobody from school living in my street. Nobody to see the stupid blue bus turn up each morning to take Alex to school. Nobody knows about him. Don't you see?'

I don't see, not really. I've spent my whole life longing for a brother or sister, someone to look after, someone to share my crazy family with. I can't imagine having one and wishing I didn't.

'Alex is cool,' I say in a small voice.

'Yes, Alex is cool!' she tells me. 'Alex is cool and cute and funny and I love him like mad. But he's hard work too, and he does crazy things, like sneaking through here to feed the birds and sit by the statue the whole time. It's not easy.'

'Suppose not,' I say.

Kristina slumps down on to the bench. 'You don't understand,' she says. 'He gets ill sometimes. He has seizures. There has to be someone with him, every minute of every day, just in case. And if you take your eye off him for a minute and he wanders off – guess who gets in trouble? He's all they think about, my mum and dad. Sometimes I think he's all they care about.'

I sink down beside her. 'You just can't keep him a secret, that's all.' I shrug. 'He's a person. He's too big to hide.'

'You don't get it, do you?' Kristina snaps. 'How could you? Little Miss Perfect, with your shiny shoes and your grade A homeworks and your perfect family. I'm not perfect, OK? I'm mean and selfish and spiteful, and yeah, I'm not proud of it, but sometimes my brother embarrasses me. Happy now? How could you possibly understand what that's like?'

There's a silence, broken only by a soft, snuffling sound, and I realize with a jolt that Kristina Kowalski is crying. I unzip my rucksack, dig out a packet of tissues and hand them over. I can hear her sniffing and sobbing in the dark beside me.

'I'm not perfect, either,' I reply, and Kristina gives a snorting laugh, but I keep talking. 'Nor is my family. You remember my gran and grandad from Parents' Night, don't you? Kind of embarrassing, yeah?'

'Too right,' Kristina says.

I shrug. 'Well, Gran's got problems – she's got that old-people illness, Alzheimer's. She gets confused. Sometimes she wanders off too. So I do understand about Alex, just a little bit.'

'Maybe,' Kristina says, blowing her nose.

'Trust me,' I tell her. 'My family's about as far from perfect as it's possible to get. You haven't met my dad, but I bet you saw him in the papers last week – *Elvis Impersonator Wows City Councillors*. He did a gig at a council banquet, and got his picture taken with the Lord Mayor. He was wearing a bright blue catsuit, sunglasses and more gold chains than the Mayor.'

'That's your dad?' Kristina gawps.

I tell her about Victoria too, and the Scottish wedding scheduled for April Fool's Day, with me dressed up as a 1960s bridesmaid.

'Eeeughh,' Kristina sniffs. 'Why are you telling me all this?'

'Because I'm sorry if I made you feel bad about keeping Alex a secret,' I explain. 'I don't think it's the right thing to do, but hey, I'm a fine one to talk. I keep my family secret too. I don't want people to laugh at them. I don't want people to laugh at *me*. I guess that makes us even.'

'I've been stupid, haven't I?' Kristina says, dabbing at her eyes.

'Yeah well, I've been stupid too.'

And then, somehow, I forget that the mud-spattered, snivelling girl next to me is Kristina Kowalski, lippy, hard-faced Year Eight siren. I tell her stuff I've never told anyone – about Mum, about the drink and the stealing and the night in the police cells, about just how far from perfect my family really is.

We sit together on the bench in front of the

statue of Our Lady of Sorrows, and somewhere along the line Kristina hands the tissues back to me because I'm crying now, fat tears of shame and fear rolling down my cheeks in the dark. When I've told her all of it, she puts an arm around me and tells me it'll be OK, and although I know that probably isn't true, it helps. It helps to know that someone cares.

'I won't tell anyone,' Kristina whispers.

I smile into the darkness. 'No, but maybe I will,' I say. 'One day. It doesn't have to be a secret, does it?'

Kristina shakes her head.

'I won't tell anyone either,' I promise. 'About Alex. It's up to you.'

'Thanks, Jude,' she says. 'You're OK, you are. For a geek.'

I look up at the statue of Our Lady of Sorrows. Her face is still sad, beautiful, marble-cool, but as I sit on the bench in the dark with Kristina Kowalski, I'd swear I can see her smile.

'Thank you, Miss Reilly, you can go now.'

I take a deep breath in and thank the examiner, and he nods and smiles and writes on his clipboard as I bolt out of the room. It's over, and it went OK. I am light-headed with relief.

Miss Lloyd is waiting on the soft chairs outside.

'That was great, Jude, from what I heard. Well done!'

'Think I passed?' I ask.

'I'm sure of it,' Miss Lloyd says. 'Flying colours.'

'Well, my scales weren't perfect, and the sight reading was slow . . .'

'You passed,' Miss Lloyd insists. 'I'm sure of it.'

I hand her a small package, wrapped in tissue paper. It's a bag of fudge from the corner shop, not the box of chocolates I wanted her to have, but I've made it look as special as I can.

'Oh Jude, no need for that,' Miss Lloyd beams. 'But thank you!'

'Thank *you*,' I reply. 'I have to go now – Grandad will be waiting.'

'Of course – the wedding!' Miss Lloyd says. 'Come on, let's get you downstairs . . . and well done again!'

We walk down the concrete stairs and push through the double doors, out into the cool evening air. No Grandad.

'I can wait with you,' Miss Lloyd says. 'No trouble.'

'There's no need,' I tell her. 'Grandad's meeting me at quarter to six, and it's still only twenty to – no need to worry.'

'Well, if you're sure . . . I might just catch the music shop. They're open till six on a Friday!' Miss Lloyd pats my arm proudly, winks and walks briskly away.

I check my watch. Five forty-two. I scan the crowded pavements, still glowing with the adrenalin buzz of the exam. Grandad knows exactly where we're meeting – I pointed it out from the bus last week. Plenty of time.

'Jude!' Mum is weaving along the busy pavement, in and out of the shoppers, with her red shoes and her pink leather jacket and Toto loping ahead of her on the lead. In spite of everything, my heart soars. She's come to see how I did.

'Mum! I didn't expect to see you here! It went well, I think. A few little mistakes, but apart from that . . .'

'What?' Mum looks puzzled. 'Oh. The exam. Well, that's good. Come on, then, Jude, we can't hang about all night . . .'

She hooks an arm through mine and tries to pull me forward, but I shake her off. 'No, Mum, I'm waiting for Grandad, remember?' I say. 'We're going to the station.'

Mum laughs, shaking her head. 'No, no, change of plan,' she says. 'Dad couldn't make it, so I said I'd take you. Now, let's get going!' She marches off along the crowded pavement, leaving me to run along behind.

'Why couldn't Grandad make it?' I demand. 'What's happened?'

'Nothing's happened, he just asked if I'd do it,' she says. 'Come on!'

My head is buzzing. Why did Grandad ask Mum to do it? Isn't he feeling well? Or Gran, maybe? Grandad wouldn't ask Mum to help out if he could help it, not the way she is right now.

'Is Gran sick?' I ask. 'Or Grandad? Tell me!'

'Everybody's fine,' Mum insists. 'Honestly, Jude! Just hurry!'

We cut down through the subway and up again on to the path that leads to the station. Toto stops to pee in a flower bed set out with tulips and daffodils arranged in straight lines, but Mum yanks him onwards.

'Just see me on to the train,' I tell her. 'You don't have to come to Birmingham – I can manage the change fine. If I get confused, I'll ask someone.'

'It's all arranged.'

'You can't take Toto on the train!' I argue, clutching at straws.

'You can,' Mum tells me. 'It's not a problem. I know what I'm doing!'

I wish I believed that. We sweep into the station with twenty minutes to spare. 'Look after the dog,' Mum says. 'I need a ticket.'

'You've got one, haven't you?' I say. 'Grandad's one. What's the problem?'

'I've forgotten it, haven't I?' Mum snaps. 'Wait there.'

I sink down on to a bench, Toto at my feet, while Mum joins the long queue. People swarm through the turnstiles, tired, coats flapping, briefcases and carrier bags swinging, home from work. Others guard their suitcases, studying the departures board, or choose a magazine for their journey.

A group of boys move away from the front of the ticket queue, gliding gracefully across the shiny marble floor of the station concourse, hockey sticks in hand. It's Brendan, Carter and a bunch of other kids from school – the street hockey team – and they're on Rollerblades. They swoop and skid through the crowd of commuters, laughing and shouting and batting a squashed-up Coke can back and forth between them.

'Oy, lads!'

A couple of station officials run forward, trying to break up the Coke-can game, but the bladers are too quick, too clever. They shoot forward, tickets ready, and disappear through the ticket barriers on to the platform. All except Carter.

The officials have cornered him somewhere near the magazine stall, backing him up against the wall. A small crowd of onlookers watch, amused. I can't hear what the station officials are saying, but it's obviously some kind of warning. Carter is trying to argue, but the officials stay stern. Finally, he bends down, pulls off his Rollerblades and flings them down on to the shiny marble floor in a temper.

They slide off in different directions, one right into the path of a fresh batch of commuters. A suited businessman stops short, blinks at the Rollerblade, then kicks it out of his way. It comes to a halt at my feet. Toto sniffs at it, suspiciously, then backs off.

The station officials have finished with Carter, and he's looking around, crestfallen, for his blades. He picks one up, scans the station concourse and finally sees me, sitting quietly with an Afghan hound and a Rollerblade at my feet.

'Jude,' he says, pink-faced. 'Please tell me you didn't see that.'

'See what?'

'You're lying, aren't you?' he asks, stricken. 'You saw everything. Why am I such an idiot?'

'You want me to answer that?'

'Just my luck,' he says, flopping down on to the bench beside me. Toto, not known for his manners, starts snuffling at Carter's socks.

'Hey,' he protests. 'They were clean on yesterday!'

'This is Toto,' I explain.

'Hi, Toto.' He offers his hand for Toto to sniff, and is rewarded with a swift lick. 'Look, he likes me! Clever dog. Looks like I've missed my train, now, anyway. We had a match fixed up out in Canley – good job I was only the reserve.'

'Have you ever thought of trying a different hobby?' I ask. 'One you're actually good at?'

Carter looks puzzled. 'Where's the challenge in that?'

'Just a thought,' I say.

Carter shrugs. 'Wasn't it your piano exam today?'

'Yup. It went OK.'

''Course it did! You practise all the time! Too much, probably. You should practise less and hang out with me, it'd give your playing a bit of edge.'

'You think?'

'I think. Definitely.' His hazel eyes twinkle.

'You need to practise all the time to get good at something,' I tell him.

'I know,' Carter says. 'All I'm saying is, practise something different. Practise hanging out with me. Like you say, we'd get pretty good at it, eventually.'

'Hanging out is not a skill,' I argue. 'You just do it.'

'So just do it!'

I roll my eyes, exasperated. Carter takes out a half-eaten chocolate bar. He offers me a bit, scoffs the rest, then scribbles something in pencil on the back of the wrapper and hands it to me.

'What's this?' I ask, squinting at the six numbers scrawled across the chocolate-stained paper.

'In case you want to call me over the weekend,' Carter says carelessly. 'Practise hanging out. Or whatever.'

'Whatever,' I laugh, pocketing the crumpled chocolate wrapper. Mum has left the ticket queue and is making for the magazine stall, her red shoes making a clickety-click sound on the cool marble floor.

'So. Where are you going?' Carter wants to know. 'Tea out in Birmingham, as a treat? Front-row tickets for a symphony orchestra? Cruft's dog show?'

I think about Kristina Kowalski, mystery girl, only child, cold, sharp-tongued Barbie-clone. Then I think of her last night, crawling through a hedge on her hands and knees, twigs in her hair, looking for a lost brother. We're a little bit the same, Kristina and me. We edit the truth, keep stuff hidden, awkward stuff, embarrassing stuff. We're trying to be normal, ordinary, average, terrified someone will find out different.

What's the point? Suddenly, it all seems like way too much effort.

I sigh. 'I'm going to Scotland for my dad's wedding.'

Carter opens his eyes wide. 'What, your dad who had the weird Elvis New Year party?' he says, frowning.

'He's marrying his girlfriend,' I explain. 'Victoria. She was the one in the black beehive wig. They're – um – kind of carrying on the Elvis theme.'

'Seriously?' Carter asks. 'An Elvis wedding? No way!'

'Way,' I tell him.

'Cool!' he breathes. 'Are you a bridesmaid, then? You'll have to show me the photos!'

'There'll be no photos,' I say sternly. 'And you are not to tell anyone at school about this. OK?'

Carter just shakes his head and laughs, and tells me his lips are sealed, for now at least. What's it worth, he wants to know, to keep it that way? In the distance, Mum approaches, clutching a carrier bag of supplies. Toto jumps up, tail wagging, as she reaches us.

'Ready, Jude?' she asks, and I'm certain that only I can hear the slight slur as she speaks. We stand up, and I can sense Carter clocking the pink leather jacket, the too-short skirt, the orange-blonde hair with months of roots showing. He'll be breathing in the scent of face-powder and hairspray, the smouldering ciggy, missing the faint, sweet smell of whisky. I hope.

'Who's this then, Jude?' Mum asks, brightly. 'Boyfriend, is it?'

Carter's grin is wider than his face.

'No, it isn't,' I snap. 'Mum, this is Kevin Carter, from school. Carter, this is my mum.'

'Hello, Mrs Reilly.' He beams, offering a hand for Mum to shake. 'Pleased to meet you at last!'

There's a crackling, muffled announcement on the tannoy, and I look at my watch. 'Mum, quick, that's our train!'

We sprint for the ticket barriers, hurtle across the platform, a muddle of school bag, red stilettos, skittering Afghan hound. 'See you Monday!' Carter shouts, but I don't have time to reply.

The guard bundles us into the last open doorway before slamming it shut behind us and blowing the whistle. We fall into the nearest empty seats, Toto curling up at our feet.

Mum dumps her bag down on the table. It's the big pink one, not the little shoulder bag, and it looks surprisingly full. She starts unpacking magazines, sandwiches, chocolate, water, cans of pop. There's enough to keep a small army fed and entertained. I frown.

'You're only coming with me as far as Birmingham,' I say.

Mum laughs, and the sound is like glass breaking, a thin, splintering sound, yet musical.

'Oh no, Jude,' she says. 'Is that what you thought? No, I'm coming *with* you. All the way to Gretna Green.'

We've done the Birmingham change and we've been on the Carlisle train for ages. I've tried praying for snow on the line, engine trouble, signal failure, earthquake. Nothing happens. We stop at Lancaster, and I think about making a run for it, but hey, Mum would probably carry on without me.

If I had a mobile phone, I could call home, speak to Grandad, find out what is going on. I could call Dad and Victoria, tell them, warn them. I could do *something*.

Toto knows I'm upset, and rests his head in my lap. I feed him slivers of ham from my sandwich, crusts, crisps, squares of chocolate. I stroke his silky, crimped ears while Mum sips mini-bottles of wine from the buffet car and flicks at her silver lighter, trying to get it to fire up and light her ciggy.

'Think I need a new one,' she grumbles. 'It's useless, this.'

The lighter flares up suddenly, igniting her ciggy and almost setting her fringe alight. 'Stupid thing!' she moans.

The man across the aisle leans over and tells her that smoking is not allowed on any part of the train. Mum tells him to mind his own business, but she puts the ciggy out anyway after a couple of puffs.

'I'm not bothered, anyway,' she says. 'We're nearly there.'

'Why are you doing this, Mum?' I ask her. 'What will Dad and Victoria think?'

'Who cares?' Mum snaps. 'It's a free country. I can go wherever I want.'

'But why would you *want* to go to Dad and Victoria's wedding?'

Mum just smiles, drains her plastic glass and leans her head back against the headrest.

Sadly, there are no earthquakes and the train rolls into Carlisle dead on time. We grab our stuff and spill out on to the platform, and Toto lifts his leg and pees against the train.

Dad and Victoria are waiting on the platform, faces creased with anxiety. Dad is wearing his black fringy catsuit and Victoria is turning heads in a turquoise minidress.

'Jude!' Dad yells. 'Jude, over here! We've been worried sick.' He wraps me in a quick,

rhinestone-studded hug. 'Are you OK, sweetheart?'
he whispers. 'She's drinking again, isn't she?
What a nightmare. Why on earth didn't you say
something, Jude?'

'Dunno,' I say.

I stayed silent because that way I could pretend
it wasn't happening, and also because I didn't
want the worry, the shame of it all to seep out,
spoiling Dad and Victoria's special time.

'Oh, Jude,' Dad says.

Then he looks at Mum, and his face hardens.
'Rose,' he says. 'What the hell is going on?'

She tries to flounce straight past, but Dad
catches her arm and pulls her round. It's like
pulling the string on a party popper – she
explodes, just as loud, just as colourful. She's
shouting at Dad, swearing at him, telling him to
leave her alone. Victoria puts an arm around me
gently, pulling me and Toto to one side.

'Sorry, Victoria,' I mutter. 'I tried to stop her!'

'Jude, it's not your fault! It'll be OK, you'll see.'

Right now, though, I don't think that anything
will ever be OK again.

'Don't you ever think of anyone except
yourself?' Dad is shouting. 'Twelve years on, and
you're still playing games, still telling lies. It's
pathetic, Rose!'

'I'm not playing games!' she argues.

'No?' Dad says coldly. 'Patrick called us at the hotel. You told him the exam venue had changed, left him standing on his own outside a deserted church hall in Earlsdon! He waited an hour, Rose, before he realized you'd just spun him a line. He's been worried sick!'

A clump of people have stopped to watch the row. They seem to think it's some kind of performance art or street theatre.

'What are you staring at?' Mum shouts at them, and they grab their bags and hurry away. I wish I could do that.

'I wanted to bring Jude up to Scotland,' she flings at Dad. 'Is that so bad? She's my daughter!'

'So act like a mother, then!' Dad snaps. 'Act like a daughter! You can't just go telling lies and changing plans and scaring everybody half to death. Don't you realize that?'

'I'll call Dad,' Mum says, grudgingly. 'I was going to, obviously.'

'Obviously. What are you doing here, Rose? It was all over between us years ago, you know that. What's this all about?'

Mum just laughs. 'You think it's all about you, don't you?' she says. 'You think I've come all this way to stop you from marrying that . . . that . . . *bank clerk*. Don't flatter yourself, Bobby! You're history.'

'So what *are* you doing here?' Dad persists.

'I told you,' Mum says coldly. 'I'm looking after my daughter. You expected her to travel up here alone, in the middle of the night? I don't think so!'

'We had it all arranged,' Dad protests. 'Patrick was taking her as far as Birmingham, we were meeting her here . . .'

'And anything could have happened in between!' Mum rages. 'She's only thirteen, for heaven's sake! What kind of a father are you?'

Dad looks embarrassed, guilty. 'Well, it wasn't an ideal arrangement, but . . .'

'Look, Bobby,' Mum says in a martyred tone. 'I thought I was doing everyone a favour – looking after Jude. I'm not interested in your wedding. Tomorrow I'm planning to see an old friend who lives up this way – Gina. I'll stay out of your way, don't worry. On Sunday morning, I'll take Jude home.'

'Gina?' Dad frowns, glancing at me.

I shrug. I've never heard of her, either.

'She used to work at the Irish Centre in Coventry, years ago,' Mum snaps. 'She moved to Scotland. Look, Bobby, I may not have gone about this the right way, but Dad's been such an old fusspot lately, ever since . . .'

She trails off abruptly, unsure of whether my

dad has been told about the police cell incident. 'Well, anyway, I was only trying to do the right thing for Jude, OK? And have a little break for myself too. I didn't mean to worry everyone!'

Dad sighs. 'You'll call Patrick?' he says.

'Of course. Look, I've misjudged things, I can see that, but I didn't mean to upset anybody, really. I'm trying to help. Dad's got enough on his plate looking after Mum without running around the country making sure Jude gets to your wedding – but when I suggested helping out, he got all huffy, so I told a little white lie about the exam venue to put him off the trail. I'm just trying to do my bit, honestly!'

By lying to everyone, worrying them all sick? Yeah, right.

Mum looks shamefaced. 'I'm sorry,' she says. 'It seemed like a good idea at the time – do the good mum/daughter thing and see Gina too. Don't worry, I'll stay away from the wedding. Trust me, it's really not my scene.'

'Well,' Dad says. 'I suppose. If you'd just explained . . .'

'We were worried, that's all,' Victoria says.

Mum's lip curls into a sneer, and she looks at Victoria as if she's a large, unpleasant turquoise-coloured slug.

'So,' Mum says. 'Where do we get the connection to Gretna Green?'

Dad rolls his eyes. 'Rose, don't be silly. We're here to collect Jude – you may as well get a lift too.'

Mum looks unimpressed. 'In a pink Cadillac? How embarrassing. I hate flash cars. Still, if it's here . . .'

She snatches my hand and drags me up the stairs and over the bridge that leads to the exit, Toto lunging on ahead. Dad and Victoria trail along behind us, exasperated. Mum raises one unimpressed eyebrow at the pink Cadillac parked up behind the taxi rank, glinting and gleaming in the street lights.

'How was the exam, Jude?' Dad asks, unlocking the car. 'Did you play well?'

'Good of you to ask,' Mum says, even though she forgot to ask herself, earlier. 'But then, I forgot, you're only a part-time father, aren't you, Bobby?'

The piano exam seems about a million years ago, something from another lifetime. 'It was OK,' I tell Dad, in a small voice.

Mum slides into the back seat. Toto and I scramble in beside her. 'Nice,' she says. 'You certainly know how to live, Bobby. Of course, the money it's costing to hire this old crate could keep your daughter in piano lessons for a year . . .'

Dad sighs, heavily. 'I'll talk to the hotel,' he says. 'We've booked a twin room for Jude, just along the corridor from us. They'll probably let you stay too, if I explain things. You'll have to sneak Toto in, though.'

Toto, hearing his name, starts to whine.

'Is he OK?' Victoria asks, as Dad starts the engine and slides the pink Cadillac out into the traffic. 'The dog?'

'Don't know,' I mumble. 'It was a long train journey.'

And Toto, who has spent the last few hours eating crisps, crusts, ham and chocolate, moans gently and pukes all over the candy-coloured carpet.

'Oh, Toto, not in the lovely pink car,' Mum croons. 'Naughty!' But when I look at her in the dark I can see she's grinning, like it's the funniest thing she ever saw.

I feel like I've slept for a hundred years. I wake slowly, my head fuzzy, wrapped in a blanket of dread.

Toto is stretched out beside me, head on the pillow. He twitches and whimpers in his sleep, chasing rabbits maybe, or cats. Mum opens the curtains and turns to face me, munching toast.

'Come on, Jude,' she says, brightly. 'We don't want to be late.'

I close my eyes again, remembering. When we arrived at the hotel, Dad checked us in. The lobby was crowded with partygoers, and Mum walked across it in her red shoes, head held high, with Toto loping ahead of her like a film star's dog. Nobody stopped them.

I remember pouring water into a saucer for Toto, feeding him custard cream biscuits from beside the kettle. My travel bag was there already, the candyfloss dress hanging up in a blur of pink.

I rang Grandad from the hotel phone, but Mum wouldn't speak to him.

'Tell him I was only trying to help,' she sniffed.

'You tell him,' I said, but she just reached into the minibar and pulled out a whisky miniature. I told Grandad I loved him, and Gran, then slipped under the covers and fell into sleep.

It's past ten o'clock.

'Why didn't you wake me?' I wail, stumbling out of bed.

'I told you it was late,' Mum says, smugly. 'Come *on*!' She pushes the bridesmaid's dress into my arms, shoves me towards the bathroom.

I seem to have slept in my clothes. I peel off crumpled school uniform and step into the shower, uncapping a bottle of complimentary hotel shampoo. The water's lukewarm, but it shocks my skin awake. At least the towels are soft and fluffy. I dig out tights and undies, slip into the dress. Red fringing swishes merrily above my kneecaps.

'Nice,' Mum says, nastily, when I venture out. 'Is this a wedding or a circus?'

Tears prick at my eyes. I rub at my hair with the hotel towel. The clock says 10.25. The wedding is just over an hour away.

'What about my hair?' I panic. 'Victoria was

going to style it for me, backcombed, with flicks!'

Mum raises an eyebrow. 'So *that's* what she wanted,' she says. 'The silly woman called at eight, wittering on about hair. I told her we'd manage ourselves. I mean, eight o'clock!'

It's Victoria's wedding day, and thanks to Mum, her bridesmaid has jumped ship. Great. 'You should have woken me!' I growl. 'I'm going to be so, so late!'

'Rubbish,' says Mum. 'I'll do your hair. It's what I do best, isn't it?'

Apart from wrecking other people's lives, yes, I guess so. Mum plugs in the hotel hairdryer and makes me hang my head upside down while she dries my hair. She produces styling gel from her handbag and sprays it through the ends, blowdrying them into a dramatic flick-up. My hair looks great.

'Make-up,' I say.

'You're far too young for make-up,' Mum huffs.

'Mum!'

I find shell-pink lippy and black eyeliner in my travel bag and Mum helps me put it on. Her hand shakes a little as she slicks the eyeliner under my lashes. It's ten past eleven.

'Shouldn't they have called for me by now?' I ask. 'Mum? Shall I ring them?'

'I told them we'd meet them there,' she says coolly, clipping on Toto's lead and picking up her pink leather jacket from the bed. 'Better get going.'

My heart is thumping. 'Mum, you can't come,' I tell her.

'Who wants to come?' She shrugs. 'I'm just *taking* you there. Get moving, Jude!'

We bundle out of the door, along the softly carpeted corridor. The lift doesn't come, so we run down the stairs, across the lobby.

'Excuse me!' the receptionist calls over. 'Is that a dog?'

'It's a llama,' Mum calls back. 'Very young one. Pedigree.'

The receptionist starts ranting about there being no need for sarcasm, and that dogs are not allowed in the hotel at any time.

'He didn't like it anyway,' Mum says. 'He's used to five-star accommodation.'

We run down the road and cross at the junction. 'It's somewhere around here,' Mum insists. 'The Old Smithy place. Not far – just over the road, apparently.' She stops, hands on hips.

'Jude!'

Andy, one of Dad's old band-mates from his long-gone Fab Four days, rounds the corner, jogging towards us. He still has the dodgy moptop haircut and the collarless suit. It looks kind of weird on a forty-something bloke, but hey, I am used to weird.

'Jude! Where have you been? Everyone's waiting!'

'A lady is entitled to be late,' Mum says.

'The bride is,' Andy corrects her. 'Not you lot. Come on!'

He grabs us by an elbow each, steering us along the pavement.

'Not going to say hello, Andy?' Mum asks, coyly. 'It's been a long time.'

'Hello, Rose,' he says grimly. 'I won't ask you what the hell you think you're doing here. I'm too polite. Just hurry!'

Just round the corner we spot the pink Cadillac, festooned with fluttering ribbons and pink net, parked on a gravel driveway beside an old building that proclaims it's the Old Smithy. Mum grabs a handful of ribbons as we rush past, ripping them off to fix on to Toto's collar.

'You're not going in,' I warn her as we push through the black doors.

'No?' Mum asks.

A sea of faces turns towards us. Some of them are dressed 1950s style, with quiffs and Teddy-boy suits and circle skirts with net petticoats, some are dressed 1960s style, with lurid shirts, skinny suits, pastel minidresses. It looks like a particularly sad and unruly fancy-dress party for the middle-aged.

A grey-haired couple I recognize as Victoria's parents huddle in a corner, looking bewildered. I know how they feel.

'Jude!' A couple of Victoria's workmates rush towards me, terrifying in matching pink-marshmallow wigs. 'Where have you been? Vic and Bobby are in the office, doing the paperwork. We've all been here since quarter past. Bobby's been ringing your room non-stop . . .'

There were no calls. I look at Mum. A small smile tugs revealingly at the corners of her lips. She must have pulled the phone jack out of the wall.

'Quick, these are your flowers . . .' Someone shoves a bouquet of white roses at me, and I clutch them, heart pounding. I'm to carry white roses, Victoria pink, I remember.

'Go on, Jude.' Andy propels me forward. 'I'll look after your mum.'

At that moment, a big wooden door opens and a tall, bespectacled man appears, Dad and Victoria behind him.

'If the guests and the groom would take their places . . .' he says, frowning slightly and ushering everyone towards a tiny, cave-like room in the distance.

'Jude, over here!' Victoria, alarming in her towering black beehive wig, frothy net veil and white sequinned minidress, grabs my hand and pulls me back. The guests file past us. 'Are you OK? What happened?'

'Mum happened. She took the phone off the hook and I slept in . . .'

Dad strides up in his new white satin catsuit. 'Nightmare,' he says. 'I'm sorry. Where is she now?'

'Andy was with her. I think he's keeping her out of the way.' I look around me, but Andy, Mum and Toto have vanished without trace.

'Good old Andy,' Dad says.

Victoria takes my hands and holds them tightly. 'It'll be OK, Jude. You're here now, and you look lovely.'

'You look great too, Victoria,' I tell her. 'Amazing.'

'The bridegroom, please!' a stern Scottish voice calls down from the Marriage Room. 'We're all ready!'

Dad takes off towards the cave-room, his flares crackling with rhinestones as he walks. Victoria's dad links her arm, and she pulls me up close on her other side. A wailing, yowling screech erupts, and a bearded piper steps from the shadows to pipe us along to the Marriage Room. I've never heard 'Love Me Tender' (by Elvis, of course) played on the bagpipes before.

We set off towards the cave-like room, clutching our bouquets, heads held high, the piper wailing behind us. As we approach, I can see the huge iron anvil in the middle of the little room, the rows of fancy-dress guests behind it. A few people make soft, cooing sounds, and someone at the back blows their nose loudly. When we reach the front, I squeeze Victoria's hand and let it go, moving back behind the anvil. Victoria's dad does the same.

Bobby and Victoria are centre stage now.

The caterwauling bagpipes die away, the registrar clears his throat and a hush descends on the room. Suddenly, off to our left, a shrill voice cuts into the silence.

'You can't stop me,' Mum is saying. 'I've come all this way.'

'Rose, be sensible,' Andy's voice protests. 'You don't want to do this, really you don't.'

'I do,' comes the response. 'I do, and I will. Do you think you can stop me? Get *off* me! Leave me alone!'

Victoria puts a hand over her eyes and bites her white-painted lips. Dad's shoulders slump.

'Can we have a minute?' he asks the registrar.

'A minute,' the bespectacled man says with a sigh. 'No more.'

The guests are whispering now, craning their necks to see what's going on. Dad strides out into the corridor, just as Mum and Toto march into view.

'Hello, Bobby,' she says crisply. 'Congratulations. Or should I say *April Fool*?'

'I tried to stop her!' Andy protests, hobbling into view. 'She just won't listen. She kicked me!'

The piper steps into the corridor, tactfully trying to block the scene of the disturbance from general view as he squeezes a mournful Scottish tune from the bagpipes. Sadly, I still have a perfect view over his left shoulder.

'Rose, you promised you wouldn't do this,' Dad is saying wearily.

'Promised!' Mum barks. 'Well, we all know you're not known for keeping *your* promises, don't we, Bobby? Anyway, it's not you I want to speak to. It's *her*!'

'Victoria?' Dad blinks. 'Victoria has nothing to say to you.'

'Too bad. I have something to say to *her*.'

Victoria appears at Dad's elbow, trailing clouds of white net veil. 'It's OK, Bobby,' she says softly. 'I'll talk to her.'

She walks past Dad, takes Mum by the arm and tries to steer her down the corridor, out of earshot. Mum shakes her off.

Dad walks back into the Marriage Room, clears his throat and tells the startled guests there will be a small delay. 'Five minutes?' he pleads with the registrar, who rolls his eyes and sits down on a rocky window sill. Mum has dropped Toto's lead, and he is running around the Marriage Room, sniffing excitedly, his pink ribbon bow askew.

I edge into the doorway to get a better view of Mum and Victoria – and to stop the rest of the guests doing the same.

'Bobby lets people down,' Mum is saying. She scrabbles in her bag for a cigarette, finds one and balances it on her bottom lip. 'He'll break his promises and break your heart and leave you with nothing. Don't marry him. He'll ruin your life.'

'Rose, he won't,' Victoria says gently. 'I know he won't.'

'You think you're so special?' Mum laughs, flicking her silver lighter on and off, trying to find a flame. 'You think you're so different? Don't kid yourself. You make me sick with your smug little smile and your idiotic sixties wedding! What do you think you look like?'

'Rose, please . . .'

'*Rose, please* . . .' Mum mimics, harshly, and I cringe at her nastiness. 'What are you, forty years old? Who told you this piece of tat looked good on you?' She waves a hand towards the white shimmery dress, still flicking the lighter for a flame. 'It's a joke! And this . . . this ridiculous wig! Don't you know they're all laughing at you? Darn it, what's *wrong* with this lighter?'

Suddenly, Mum's lighter flashes into life, a big blue flame leaping up from her fingertips. As we watch, the flame flashes across to Victoria's veil, searing along the frothy white net like a snake, curling, sizzling, melting.

Mum screams, Victoria screams, and then the whole place erupts.

I think I might faint with horror. Even in my wildest nightmares, I never imagined this. I can't seem to breathe, and my nostrils clog with the stink of burning nylon.

'Bobby, *quick!*' one of the pink-wigged women shrieks. 'The veil's stiff with hairspray, and so is the wig. If *that* goes up . . .'

Dad shoves past me and thunders towards the beehive inferno in a blur of white satin. The piper, meanwhile, has thrown down his bagpipes, pulled a fire extinguisher off the wall and is spraying the corridor.

It's Mum who saves the day. She grabs the smouldering wig, complete with flaming veil, wrenches it from Victoria's head and hurls it to the floor. Then she jumps on it, stamping out the flames with her pointy red shoes while the piper squirts fire-extinguisher foam all over it.

'Jesus, Rose!' Dad whispers, his face almost as ashen as my own.

But Victoria, looking strangely naked without her wig, mousy hair scraped flat and clipped out of the way, puts an arm around Mum's shaking shoulders. 'It was an accident, Bobby,' she says. 'Just an accident.'

And Mum rests her head on Victoria's shoulder and cries and cries and cries.

26

The building is evacuated, the fire brigade are called and, once everything is declared safe again, the wedding is finally rescheduled for 1.30 p.m. The advantage of getting married on April Fool's Day is that few people are stupid enough to want to, so there are hardly any other bookings. Victoria borrows a marshmallow-pink beehive wig from one of her bank-clerk friends.

'Something borrowed,' she says brightly. 'Don't think I'll bother with a veil this time!'

Her dad escorts her into the Marriage Room with me following behind, leading Toto in a haze of pink net and ribbon. The piper is absent – he offered to take Mum back to the hotel when her increasingly frantic apologies were threatening to halt the wedding for a second time.

'You're the hero of the hour,' he told her gently, politely leaving out the fact that she actually caused the blaze in the first place. 'Let me buy you a drink to calm your nerves.'

'Oh,' Mum faltered. 'Well. OK, then!'

So Victoria floats into the Marriage Room to a tinny CD version of 'Love Me Tender', which sounds a whole lot better than the bagpipe one, and the wedding goes without a hitch.

It's not a pretty ceremony, like the church weddings I've seen on TV soap operas. It's kind of plain and ordinary and thankfully quick, and before I know it the bespectacled registrar lifts up the heavy iron hammer at the foot of the anvil and lets it drop with an ear-splitting clang.

He pronounces Dad and Victoria man and wife. They pose beside the anvil and a weird flashing erupts from the wall, which panics me briefly, but it's only a camera, not Mum with her pyromaniac lighter. It's done, all over, finally, without disaster.

We straggle back along the street to the hotel, where the reception is now more than two hours overdue. 'Wasn't it lovely?' people are saying, brushing confetti from their hair as we walk along. 'Something different, something special. A real day to remember.'

Well, it was that, all right.

The pink Cadillac cruises past, tin cans, old boots and what seems to be a slightly charred white net veil tied on to the back bumper.

Back at the hotel, the manager swoops on

Toto. 'I told the lady earlier, no dogs on the premises,' he says grimly. 'We have health and safety rules, you know.'

'Can't you make an exception, just this once?' Dad asks politely. 'This dog's an important guest at the wedding, and he's travelled a long way to be here today. He's very highly trained!'

Toto is sniffing the back of the manager's trousers.

'I can't help that,' the man says primly, trying to step out of sniffing range. 'We cannot have dogs in the hotel – it's against all our rules. And your "highly trained" dog has already left a little . . . *message*, shall we say? In Room 201, behind the armchair.'

'Oops,' I say.

So Toto is shut into the pink Cadillac. His ear-splitting yowls can be heard throughout the wedding meal and the yawn-making speeches. Everyone drinks a toast in pink champagne – everyone except Victoria. And me. We stick to lemonade.

The wedding cake is a mountain of chocolate profiteroles with an Elvis action figure and a Barbie Doll with a beehive and a minidress perched on the lower slopes. Surprise, surprise, the band are Dad's old mates, the Fab Four, Andy on lead guitar, playing countless dismal songs from long, long ago. At least they drown out Toto's distant whines.

Dad and Victoria circle the dance floor, cheek to cheek. I can't help grinning. It came so close to being ruined, but everything worked out in the end. They got their special day.

'Come on, Jude!' Victoria shouts, waving at me from the dance floor. 'Please!' I smile and shake my head, but Victoria swoops down on me and I abandon any attempts at cool and join in.

It's much later when I spot Mum at the bar alone, waving madly. I pick my way towards her.

'Mum?' I shout, above the pounding sixties music. 'Is this a good idea, d'you think, being here? After what happened earlier?'

'I've made a fool of myself,' she says into her whisky. 'I feel so stupid. I'm such an embarrassment!'

Well, yeah. The smell of burning bridal veil is still scarily fresh in my memory, so it must be in Mum's too.

'Everyone makes mistakes,' I say kindly. Not everyone makes them with a dodgy lighter in their hand, of course, but I decide not to mention this.

'I'm going to change, Jude,' she tells me. 'I'll give up drinking – and smoking. I promise.'

'Yeah, right,' I say.

'Really. Jude, wake-up calls don't come any

clearer than this one. Right now, I just need to get out of here,' Mum says, and I notice for the first time that her pink holdall and my overnight bag are leaning up against the bar. 'We have to go, Jude.'

'What, now? We'll miss the rest of the party. We'll miss the fireworks!'

'I think we've had the fireworks already,' Mum says ruefully. 'Look, let me explain to your dad – then we'll go.'

There's a flash of white satin at my side. 'Explain what, Rose?' Dad asks.

Mum looks stricken. 'Well, this afternoon,' she says in a small voice. 'The accident. I behaved appallingly.'

'Yes,' Dad agrees. 'You did. Still, I guess we'll get over it.'

'I won't!' Mum declares. 'Not ever! I've learnt my lesson this time, Bobby. I'm so ashamed. I just want to get out of here, take Jude home. I should never have come in the first place.'

'No,' Dad agrees. 'It's all been a bit of a mess.'

'If I just had some cash . . .'

Dad sighs, reaching into the pocket of his satin catsuit to bring out a wad of notes. 'Sorry, Jude,' he says to me. 'It's probably for the best. They're not going let Toto stay here another night, and you can see how upset your mum is. I'd feel better if I knew you were back home.'

Mum pockets the cash. 'I knew you'd understand, Bobby. There's a train soon after six, if I can just get to Carlisle – I rang National Rail Enquiries earlier. I suppose we could get a taxi . . .'

Dad sighs. 'Vic hasn't been drinking,' he says. 'I expect she'd drive you . . .'

Half an hour later, I'm standing on the platform at Carlisle station waiting for the Birmingham train, wearing my school blazer over the pink minidress and red boots. This is not a good look, but when I took my travel bag into the station loos a few minutes back to get changed, I discovered that Mum had cleverly dumped my school bag inside, but left my neatly folded pile of 'normal' clothes back in the hotel room. Great.

'No problem,' Dad says. 'We'll bring them down for you after the honeymoon.'

'I know, but I'll be stuck like this for the whole journey . . .'

'You look lovely,' Victoria says, and I bite my tongue and try to smile. Mum, meanwhile, is still apologizing for the Burning Veil Disaster.

'Don't give it another thought, Rose,' Victoria says. 'No harm done!'

No harm done? I can practically see small, fluffy wings sprouting up from Victoria's sequinned shoulders, a halo hovering above her candyfloss wig.

Mum takes Victoria's hands, like the two of them are new best friends. 'I should never have said the things I did,' she says. 'I was angry, and bitter, and . . . well, drunk. I'm sorry. Sorry for all of it. I hope you and Bobby will be very happy.'

'Rose, you don't know what that means to me,' Victoria says, flinging her arms around Mum. I get hugged too, of course, and then Dad and Victoria grin and wave and wish us luck, and they walk away, back to their snazzy pink Cadillac, their party, the fireworks, the honeymoon.

'There's just something I need to check,' Mum says, the minute they're out of sight. She disappears into the ticket office, then emerges a minute later full of smiles, a cigarette dangling from her lip.

'Know what?' she says, between puffs. 'My life up to now has been one big disappointment. A career that flopped before it even got started, a series of no-good men –'

'Dad's not no-good!'

'Well, maybe he was just wrong for me,' Mum says. 'Life isn't like the movies, Jude. I wish it was. Is it so wrong to want romance, adventure? To want to see the world in glorious Technicolor, instead of boring black and white?'

'Well . . .'

'Jude, today was a nightmare,' she says, taking a drag on her cigarette. 'For the first time ever, I saw myself the way others see me – a sad, middle-aged woman with a drink problem, making a fool of herself in public. That's not who I want to be. I'm scared, Jude. Scared I've left it too late to have a life!'

'Don't be silly, Mum! It's never too late!'

'I knew you'd say that!' Mum grins. 'I knew you'd understand! What better chance will we ever have to get away, make a fresh start? Find our own yellow-brick road, our own Emerald City?'

She takes my hand, pulls me up the steps and over the footbridge.

'What are you doing, Mum?' I protest. 'The Birmingham train goes from platform one. It says so on the departures board . . .'

'No, no,' she says. 'We need platform three.'

A small knot of panic forms in my belly. 'Mum?'

She runs down the stairs on to the opposite platform, dragging me and Toto in her wake. The station loudspeaker system crackles into life, telling me something I don't understand, don't want to understand, about the train now standing at platform three. Then we're on the train, squishing into a table seat, Toto settling himself down in the aisle with a huff.

I look along the crowded carriage, spot the computerized information board above the door. *This train is the 18.22 for Glasgow Central*, it tells me. *This train shall call at Glasgow Central only.*

Mum turns to me. 'It's time we made our very own adventure,' she says excitedly. 'You and me, Jude!'

The train slides noiselessly forward, gathering speed, but it's taking us further and further from home.

'Mum!' I argue. 'This is crazy! What about Gran and Grandad?'

'What about them?' Mum says. 'They think we're in Gretna for another night. They won't worry.'

'But I want to go home!'

'We *will*,' Mum tells me. 'Eventually. But we're going to see Gina first.'

'Gina?'

'The old friend I told you about,' Mum says, laughing. 'The one who moved to Scotland.'

'Mum, we can't!'

'Well, this train doesn't stop again until Glasgow,' Mum points out. 'So, actually, we can. Cheer up, Jude, it'll be fun! Gina's a great girl.'

'You haven't seen her for years!'

'Well, no,' Mum admits. 'But she sent me a Christmas card with her new address.' Mum scrabbles in the pink holdall, pulls out a crumpled card with a cartoon of Santa, drunk and snoring beneath a Christmas tree.

'She looks like a great laugh,' I say sourly.

'No, no, look at the message,' Mum insists. 'Don't you see?'

I look at the curly blue biro writing. *Got a job as barmaid at a great old pub in Glasgow*, I read. *The Wizard. You'd love it, Rose!*

'See?' Mum says. 'The Wizard! Like in *The Wizard of Oz*! We can't ignore that, can we? It's an omen!'

I bite my lip. We're going to Glasgow to see a woman Mum knew slightly years ago, all because she works in a pub called The Wizard. It's an omen all right – a bad one.

'It's just a stupid film!' I say, and watch the smile slide from her face. A minute later, she is climbing over Toto, lurching her way down the carriage in search of the buffet car and more of those dinky pop-bottle sized shots of wine.

I fell for it, again. I believed her shamefaced apologies, her promises to change, but none of it meant a thing. It's still April the first, I remember. And I'm the biggest fool of all.

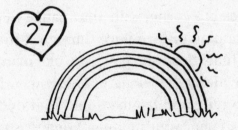

Mum sits at the piano, hammering out Irish tunes while the whole pub sings along. '"The Fields of Athenry"!' they shout, the minute one song ends. '"Molly Malone"! Come on, Rose, love!'

Mum has made two dozen new best friends. She knows every song they ask for – she should do, she's had years of practice. It never fails to amaze me how her fingers can move so quickly, so gracefully, even when she's steaming drunk. Whiskies line up on top of the piano, and she hasn't paid for a single one herself.

'Come in, come in!' Gina said when we arrived, ushering us into the darkest, dingiest pub I'd ever seen. 'What a surprise! My old mate Rose – and is this little Julie? All grown up?'

'It's Jude,' I mumbled, but I don't think she even heard.

That was hours ago. It's Saturday night and The Wizard is crammed with regulars,

Glaswegians, mostly of Irish descent. Mum, glued to the piano, is the star attraction.

I'm stuck in a corner with Toto, eating a cheese roll and sipping orange juice through a straw.

'Something Scottish, now,' an old man calls out. 'How about "I Belong to Glasgow"?' Mum knows the tune and launches into it at once.

'What a talent your mum is,' Gina says to me. 'You must be very proud, Julie.'

I bite my lip.

'Is there anything else I can get you? A piece of apple pie? Some water for the dog?'

'Is there a telephone I can use?' I ask. 'I need to call home.'

'Ah, sure there is, sweetheart. Out in the lobby there. Help yourself!'

She sorts me out with loose change and finds me the dialling code for Coventry, and I stand in the lobby shivering, pressing in the numbers. The call rings through, but there's nothing but a ringtone at the other end. Nobody picks up. I try again, but still there's no reply.

Gran and Grandad must have gone out. Perhaps they're shopping. But . . . on a Saturday night? I decide to call again later.

I slip outside, Toto at my heels. The street is deserted, except for a chip paper blowing along in the gutter and a skinny kid on a bike in the distance, doing wheelies in the light of the lamp post. Across the road, there's a rundown warehouse and a row of boarded-up shops. Toto shivers and tries to hide behind my legs. It's like a wasteland.

I go back inside. Mum has left the piano, despite the protests of her admiring audience. 'Later, OK?' she promises. 'I'll play again later.'

'Just one more?' the old man pleads.

'No, no, I'm taking a break!' Mum says. 'Maybe Jude will play something for you? She's very good. She takes after me, musically.'

I hide behind my hands.

'Come on, Jude!' Mum shouts. 'Show us what you can do!'

The crowd around the piano take up the cry, shouting, heckling. 'Come on, love! Give it a go!'

Gina steers me over to the piano, sits me down firmly. 'Go on, sweetheart,' she whispers. 'Just the one, eh?' It's a million times worse than any piano exam. My throat is dry, my fingers trembling. I can't remember what I'm supposed to do.

'Come on, then!' someone shouts.

'"Danny Boy"!' someone requests.

'"Wild Mountain Thyme"!'

I don't know those tunes – I've heard Mum play them, sure, but I don't know them well enough to play myself, not without music. I shoot

Mum a desperate look, and she grins and throws her head back and tells everyone it's time *she* had a request.

'OK, Jude. Just for me, OK?' She comes over, leans on the piano. 'You know the one.'

There is only one song Mum ever wants to hear me play – 'Over the Rainbow', from *The Wizard of Oz*. I've been playing it since I was nine years old. I know it inside out.

I bite my lip, begin to play. Straightaway, the noisy pub quietens, and Mum starts to sing. Her voice is reedy and rough around the edges, the voice of someone whose life has turned out badly, for reasons she can't quite fathom. I join in too.

My fingers are flying, my voice soaring up above the heads of the locals in The Wizard, out across the potholed roads and the boarded-up shops and the rundown warehouse, and far, far beyond.

When we finish, Mum is crying into her whisky and the pub is silent. The old man starts to clap and then the place erupts into a mess of whistles, cheers, applause. 'Lovely, sweetheart,' Gina says. 'Just lovely!'

Later, I call Grandad again, then again, just after midnight, from Gina's flat above the pub, where I'm curled up under a fleece blanket on the brown nylon sofa. There's still no reply.

In the morning, I call home again, and again there's nobody there. The phone just rings and rings.

'Mum?' I say. 'Grandad's not answering the phone. What if something's wrong?'

Mum just pulls the blanket over her head and turns her back on me. I try to think of sensible explanations for why Grandad's not picking up the phone, but I can't think of any. I begin to panic.

I've punched out Dad's phone number before I remember that he's on honeymoon, cruising the Scottish Highlands in a pink Cadillac with a bundle of tin cans tied on behind it. Who else can I call?

Nuala? Giovanni? Miss Devlin? Father Lynch?

I drop the phone abruptly, grabbing my school blazer. There in the right-hand pocket is a crumpled chocolate wrapper with a six-figure number scrawled across it. *Call me*, it says.

I dial, adding in the Coventry code, and Carter picks up the phone on the third ring.

'I'm in trouble,' I blurt. 'Will you help me? Mum went kind of off the rails a bit and we're stranded in Glasgow and nobody knows . . .'

'Slow down,' Carter says. 'I'm listening.'

'Carter, something's wrong,' I tell him. 'I know there is. Gran and Grandad won't pick up the phone – I've been ringing and ringing, and there's just no reply. Can you go round and check that everything's OK?'

'Hey, hey,' Carter says. 'Don't worry. Their phone's probably just out of order! I'll go round and give them a message, shall I?'

'Would you? Just tell him we're in Glasgow and we're fine. Well, kind of. We're staying with Mum's friend, Gina, at a flat above a pub called The Wizard, down by the docks.' I take a deep breath in, trying to stay calm.

'I'll tell them all that,' Carter promises. 'Leave it to me.'

'Thanks, Carter.'

'Jude?'

'Mmmm?'

'I don't want to be nosy,' he says. 'But what exactly are you doing in Glasgow?'

The tears come then, leaking out of the corners of my eyes like raindrops sliding down a windowpane. I find a tissue and blow my nose, loudly.

'I don't know,' I tell Carter at last. 'I just don't know.'

'Bag of crisps, love?' Gina asks, chucking a packet of Salt 'n' Vinegar across the bar. I smile and tear open the packet. Since we got here last night, I've eaten two cheese rolls, a packet of salted nuts and a Yorkie bar. It's not exactly a balanced diet, but it's something. The crisps probably count as a serving of vegetables.

'Thanks,' I say.

'Cheer up,' Gina tells me. 'It might never happen.'

'It already has,' I say. 'I mean, it's very nice here and everything . . .' I look around at the dingy, half-empty pub. It isn't nice at all, but I don't want to offend Gina. 'It's just we should be getting home. I'm worried about Gran and Grandad, and I'm missing my friends . . .'

'Ah, you'll soon settle in,' Gina says. 'Wait till your mum has got herself a job and a nice little flat, and you're at school again. You'll like Glasgow. It's a lively place. You'll soon make friends.'

'We're *not* staying here,' I say. Mum and Gina were up till all hours last night, sipping whisky and talking about the future. It involved a piano bar, a chain of hairdressing salons, an exclusive nightclub called Emerald City decorated to look like Oz, complete with yellow-brick dance floor. Mum likes to dream.

I look at her now, slumped at the piano, playing 'Over the Rainbow' so slowly it's hard to even recognize the tune.

'We're going home,' I say decisively.

'Maybe.' Gina shrugs, polishing a glass. 'Who can tell?'

I slip out into the lobby, Toto on my heels, to try home yet again on the payphone. No reply. Where are they? I try Carter's number next. There's been no reply all day there either, so I have no idea if he was able to pass my message on. It's past seven now.

This time, when I ring Carter, a small child answers.

'Hello. Is Kevin there?'

'We've been at Aunty Eileen's.'

'That's nice. Can you put Kevin on the line?'

There's a silence, then, 'I've got a wobbly tooth.'

'Lovely. Look, is your mum there?' I appeal. 'Or your dad? Can I speak to a grown-up please?'

'I'm not supposed to answer the phone,' the child says finally, and the line goes dead.

Great. No wonder Carter is slightly deranged – it's clearly a family trait. I push open the door, looking out into the street. It's dusk already – it's amazing how you lose track of time when you spend your days in a dark, smoky pub. I could swear I've been here a hundred years – every minute feels like a lifetime – but it's not even twenty-four hours yet.

Toto is whining softly. He hates the smoky pub atmosphere even more than I do. I took him out earlier on when Gina and Mum nipped along to the supermarket for bread and dog biscuits and whisky, but I don't fancy walking him on my own, in the dark. It's scary enough in the daylight.

I ruffle his fur and lead him back inside.

'All right, love?' Mum asks, glancing up from the piano. The pub is quiet, tonight. It's been practically empty all day, and even now there are only a few grim-faced men drinking Guinness, tucked away in the corner. Mum's good mood has leaked away like last night's party atmosphere.

'Can we take Toto for a walk?' I ask. 'He needs a run. It's not fair to keep him inside all day, in a strange place. He's missing home.'

Like me, I add, silently.

'Home?' Mum blinks. 'We've only just got here! It's going to be great – where's your sense of adventure?'

'I don't like it,' I say. 'And I'm worried about Gran and Grandad.'

Mum's eyes flash with anger. 'What about me, Jude?' she argues. 'Can't I have some fun for a change? I mean, I'm still living at home, at my age, looking after elderly parents. How sad is that?'

I was always under the impression that the elderly parents looked after us, but I don't say anything. Mum turns back to the piano and starts to bang out 'Over the Rainbow'. Almost at once, a bloke in the corner calls out.

'Not again!' he shouts, in between a whole bunch of words I can't repeat. 'Give it a rest, can't you? Kids, dogs, and now *The Wizard of Oz*! I came in here for a bit of peace!'

Gina pulls a face from behind the bar, but Mum's fingers freeze over the piano keys. Her lower lip trembles, like a small child after a telling off. She looks at me, shaken.

'I thought it would be different,' she says. 'I've messed up, big style. Maybe Glasgow isn't the Emerald City, after all?'

'Mum, there's no such place.' I squeeze in beside her on the piano stool, and Toto puts his head on her lap, brown eyes sorrowful. 'You were doing fine until you started drinking again. You just need to dump the whisky.'

'It's not that easy,' Mum says, staring into her glass.

'So do it anyway!' I say. 'Life isn't easy, is it?

I love you. So do Gran and Grandad, and Toto, but you don't care about us! Do you have any idea what it's like for me, watching my own mum drink her life away? It hurts! Why can't you stop? Just because giving up isn't *easy*?'

Mum's face is grey, her eyes wild. She makes a low, gasping sound, like someone trying to breathe underwater. 'I know,' she says. 'I'm sorry. I've let you down – all of you.' She puts an arm around me, pulls me close. 'Maybe I've used up all my fresh starts. My problems just follow, wherever I go.'

'Am I one of the problems?' I ask, in a small voice.

Mum's eyes open wide. 'How could you even think that?' she asks, genuinely astonished.

'Because when I was born, you started drinking heavily?' I say. 'Because you're so full of regrets for what might have been? And that's just a polite way of saying that things might have been different if I'd never been born. Isn't it?'

Mum's whisky glass slides through her fingers and drops to the floor, where the liquid spills out. The glass rolls into a corner, behind the piano.

'No,' she says, her face white. 'No, no, *no*. If I've ever made you feel that way . . . oh, God, I'm sorry!'

'I just thought . . .'

Mum takes my hands, holds them tight. 'No, Jude,' she whispers. 'You're the best thing that ever happened to me – the only good thing, I sometimes think. I love you. I've been stupid, always looking for things that don't exist. I don't notice what I've got, right here under my own nose.'

'You're not drinking because of me?' I ask, finally finding the courage to say it out loud. 'It's not my fault?'

Mum folds me into a bony, whisky-scented hug. 'Never, Jude,' she says. 'I drink because of *me*. Because I'm not good enough at anything I try to do – even the basic stuff, like being a mum, a daughter, a girlfriend. I want to be perfect, but I'm a mess. And sometimes, when I drink, I can kid myself that I'm not.'

She pulls away, trying for a smile.

'I don't care about perfect,' I tell her. 'I just want you. Can we go home, Mum? Please?'

'First thing in the morning,' Mum promises. 'If we had a real wizard handy, I'd wish us back right now, but like you said, that's just a stupid film. There's no such thing as magic.'

'Maybe you're just looking for it in the wrong places?'

Like at the bottom of a whisky glass.

'Maybe.'

She takes a tissue out of her bag and dabs at her eyes. I wish I could make things better, turn the world from black and white to full-on Technicolor for her, because I honestly think that real life has got its own magic. You find it in little things, unexpected things, like a tube of Love Hearts sweets, a boy feeding birds from the breadcrumbs in his palm, a plump woman in a pink wig who says it doesn't matter even when someone has just fried her bridal veil to a crisp.

Magic. It's what makes life bearable.

Suddenly, far in the distance, I hear the sound of an ice-cream van jingle, getting closer. It sounds familiar – very familiar. Mum jumps up, her face shining with hope.

'An ice-cream van, now, is it?' the grumpy man in the corner huffs. 'Can a man get no peace? Is it too much to ask?'

'Strange,' Gina says from the bar. 'An ice-cream van, at this time of night!'

Mum's eyes are dancing, but I beat her to the door. We're all on the pavement when Giovanni's van pulls up outside The Wizard, and Toto's tail is thrashing about with delight.

'What were you saying about magic?' I grin.

'This old wreck?' Mum scoffs, but she's smiling, and when Giovanni slides the door across and jumps down on to the pavement, she flings her arms round him like she hasn't seen him in a year. 'I'm sorry, Giovanni,' she's gabbling. 'So, so sorry.'

'All right, Rosa,' he says. 'It doesn't matter now.'

'Is this The One With No Backbone?' Gina wants to know, wiping her hands on her skirt. 'Forget backbone. He's cute!'

But Giovanni isn't smiling, and gently he unpeels Mum's arms from round his neck, puts a finger to her lips.

'Get your bags, Jude,' he says to me.

'OK.' I grin. 'They're just upstairs. Giovanni, how did you know we were here? How did you find us?'

His face is grim. 'Please, get your bags now,' he says. 'We have to hurry.'

'Ah, now, why don't you just come in and relax and stay the night?' Gina wants to know. 'After that long drive. The motorway will still be there in the morning!'

I cut across her babble, shivering suddenly.

'Giovanni, what's wrong?'

He takes a breath in, pushes a hand through his blue-black hair.

'It's your gran,' he says to me, softly. 'It's Molly. She's in the hospital. She's had a stroke.'

Giovanni drives through the night. We sit huddled into the cab of the ice-cream van, following distant tail lights along an endless stretch of motorway.

'What happened, Giovanni?' Mum wants to know. 'How bad is it?'

'It's bad,' he tells her. 'Patrick is at the hospital with her. He won't leave her side.'

'Oh, God,' says Mum. 'I've been such a useless daughter. Hopeless. Hopeless daughter, hopeless mum, hopeless girlfriend.'

'No,' I soothe her. 'Not hopeless at all.'

Well, maybe a little bit.

'I don't know how to thank you,' Mum tells Giovanni. 'You're my hero – the best, bravest man I ever knew. If it hadn't been for you . . .'

Giovanni shakes his head in the darkened cab. 'It's the kid with the skates you should really thank,' he says.

'What kid?' Mum puzzles. 'What skates?'

It turns out that after my phone call this morning, Carter took off and bladed round to our house to find out why Gran and Grandad weren't answering their phone. There was nobody in, so he found a neighbour who told him about the stroke, about the ambulance with its wailing siren and flashing lights. It happened on Saturday night, as Mum and Toto and I sat on a train, hurtling towards Glasgow.

'This kid, he skated right over to the hospital, found out which ward Molly was on,' Giovanni says. 'Patrick was there, of course. Your friend passed on the message, Jude, and Patrick sent him to the restaurant to find me. I was washing dishes, as usual, when this crazy kid flew into the kitchen, shouting about hospitals and phone calls and a pub in Glasgow called The Wizard . . .'

'Bet your boss liked that,' Mum says.

'He's not my boss any more.'

'Oh dear.'

I think of a boy, a lanky, straw-haired boy in scruffy school uniform, blading about the streets of Coventry on a secret mission when he should have been at his Aunty Eileen's. I think of him carrying his Rollerblades through the hushed hospital corridors in his stocking feet, bursting into the kitchen at Mario's Italian restaurant, getting chucked out again with a torrent of Italian abuse ringing in his ears.

'He's a good kid, though,' Giovanni tells me. 'He came back to the hospital with me, waited while I spoke to Patrick. He wanted to come to Glasgow too, but of course I couldn't take the time to track down his parents, clear it with them. I had to get going, find you, bring you back.'

There's a silence.

'She will be all right, though?' Mum asks. 'Won't she? People get better from strokes, don't they?'

'I can't tell you that, Rosa.' Giovanni sighs. 'We have to just hope and pray.'

I lean my head against the ice-cream van's rattly window, look out into the starless sky. I hope and I pray and, eventually, I sleep.

The ice-cream van takes up two parking spaces in the hospital car park, but it's barely four in the morning, so the place isn't exactly packed. We get out, shiver in the cold morning air.

'Stay, Toto,' I tell him, winding the passenger window down a bit and slamming the door. 'Sorry. Hospitals and dogs don't mix.'

He sticks his head out of the window, whining softly as we walk away, his crimped strawberry-blonde hair fluttering in the breeze.

It's way too early for visitors, of course, but Mum and Giovanni don't care about rules. They haul me across the hospital reception area, call the lift. We get out on the second floor.

A passing nurse frowns quizzically at us. OK, at me. I'm still in the pink minidress with the red winkle-picker boots. She probably thinks they're taking me to the psychiatric wing.

'Molly has a room of her own,' Giovanni tells us. 'This is the ward. She should be . . . just along here.'

We creep along the carpeted corridor, pause in the doorway of Room Six. In the half-light, I see Gran, sleeping, in a high hospital bed with a white waffle coverlet. When I look closely, I see that the right-hand side of her face seems to have slipped, fallen, so that it no longer matches the left side. It's scary, distorted, like a jigsaw someone has tried to force together even though the pieces are wrong.

In a soft chair at the side of the bed, Grandad is sleeping. His clothes are crumpled, his shoes discarded and kicked to one side. His head lolls and his breathing is dry and raspy, as though he's the one who's ill.

Mum sits down gently on the edge of the bed, takes Gran's hand. 'Mum, I'm sorry, so sorry,' she whispers. 'You have to get better, d'you hear? We can't do without you. *I* can't do without you.'

Grandad stirs, rustling out of sleep. 'You found them,' he says. 'Good boy, Giovanni.'

I fling my arms round Grandad, hold on tight. He smells warm and safe, like home. His rough whiskers scratch my cheek and a damp patch appears in my hair. I pull away, puzzled. Grandad doesn't cry.

'They keep telling me to go home,' Grandad says brokenly. 'Do they really expect me to do that? Leave her here, in this place? We've never been apart in fifty years.'

'I know, Patrick,' Giovanni says. 'I know.'

Abruptly, a nurse comes in, hands on hips.

'What's going on?' she asks, sternly. 'You shouldn't be here! Mr Reilly, we're breaking the rules already by allowing you to stay! Your wife is very ill, she's not up to so many visitors, and certainly not at this hour of the night. Patients are trying to sleep!'

Grandad bows his head, defeated, but Giovanni speaks up. 'We've come a long way,' he tells the nurse. 'All the way from Glasgow, driving through the night. This is Molly's daughter and granddaughter. Please – can they stay, just for a little while? Please?'

The nurse softens, smiles. 'Well. Just five minutes then, no longer,' she says. 'And quietly, OK? If Sister catches you, I'll be in big trouble!'

'Five minutes,' Giovanni promises, and the nurse turns away.

At that moment Gran's eyes flutter open. Her milky-blue eyes blink and focus, and a single tear wells and rolls down her left cheek.

'Don't, don't, Molly, pet,' Grandad says. 'I'm here. Rose is here too, and Jude, and Giovanni. We'll get you home soon, I promise you. They're doing all they can.'

Mum reaches forward to smooth Gran's hair, which lies spread across the pillow, dull, frizzy, lifeless. 'We'll get you smartened up, Mum,' she says softly. 'Good as new.'

She takes a brush from her shoulder bag and begins to brush, smoothing out the tangles so gently, so carefully, as if she's brushing spun silver. She makes a braid, weaving the hair over and under into a thick, glossy plait that curves across the white waffle coverlet like a rope of silk.

'There,' she whispers. 'All done.'

'I really must ask you to go now,' the little nurse says, reappearing in the doorway. 'Mr Reilly, you can stay, but that's all, I'm sorry. Come back later, at visiting time.'

'Rosa?' Giovanni prompts, and Mum dips down quickly, kissing Gran, backing away. I lean down next, my lips brushing the dry skin of her cheek.

'Bye, Gran,' I whisper. 'I love you. We'll be back later, promise.'

We are. Later, at visiting time, we're lined up outside the ward, rested, showered, changed, carrying flowers and chocolates and grapes and cards. We're there, ready and waiting, but even as I see the little nurse from earlier walking towards us, face fixed into a mask of sympathy, regret, I know that we're too late.

'I'm sorry,' she says, spreading her arms out and herding us into a side room. 'I tried to call you, but you must have left already. I'm very sorry to tell you that Mrs Reilly passed away, just after 12.30 p.m. It was another stroke, a massive one. It was very quick.'

I sink down on to a soft chair. A stroke. It sounds so soft, so gentle. It doesn't sound like a way to die.

'No,' Mum says. 'No, no, no!' She makes a strangled sound, slumps against Giovanni. His arm folds around her, and I see the glint of tears in his eyes.

'Mr Reilly was with her at the end,' the nurse is saying. 'She wasn't alone.'

But we are, now, without her.

I get to ride in the pink Cadillac one more time. I sit very still, my cheek against the cool, shiny glass, snuggled into the Barbie pink leather of the seats.

Gran would have liked this car. 'Ooh,' she'd have said. 'Pink to make the boys wink!'

'OK, Jude?' Dad asks.

I just nod, because I can't trust myself to speak, and Grandad, sitting beside me, covers my hand with his big rough one.

Dad and Victoria called from Killiecrankie on Monday night – they'd been calling the whole time, apparently, to check that we got home safely. When they found out about Gran, they abandoned their honeymoon tour of the Highlands and drove straight home.

'No, no, Bobby,' Grandad had insisted. 'There's nothing you can do – nothing anyone can do.'

'We can be there for you,' Dad had replied.

He was too, him and Victoria. They contacted the funeral home, organized the flowers, spoke to Father Lynch about the service. They organized all the awful, necessary jobs you have to do when somebody dies, and they did it quietly, gently, without any fuss.

Where was Mum? Well, she cried and raged and drank whisky all Monday night, with Giovanni at her side, holding her hand. For the first time in her life, she said, the drink didn't soften the edges, dull the pain.

In the morning, she hugged me and she hugged Grandad, and Giovanni drove her to the hospital. She checked herself into the alcohol dependency unit, and she's been there ever since. She's been through the initial withdrawal, and she looks more determined than I've ever seen her. She says she can do it, really kick the drink, this time.

Well, maybe.

Dad parks the pink Cadillac neatly in the car park at the church of Our Lady of Sorrows. Giovanni's ice-cream van is already parked in the corner, near the shrine. He's been to fetch Mum from the hospital. He lifts her down from the passenger seat, slides a protective arm around her. She looks too thin, too frail, as if the life has drained out of her. In the cool spring sunshine, her skin is tinged with yellow.

After the funeral service and the burial, she will have to go back to the hospital.

'Oh, Mum!' I fall into her arms.

'Hey, hey,' she whispers into my hair. 'It's OK, Jude. Seriously.'

It feels like nothing is ever going to be OK again.

'Hello, Bobby, Victoria,' she says. 'Jude's told me everything you've been doing to help. Thank you – both of you.'

'It was the least we could do,' Dad says.

'No,' Mum corrects him. 'It was much more than that.'

We walk up the church steps, Mum and Giovanni, Dad and Victoria, me and Grandad and Toto.

'Are you sure, Father Lynch?' Grandad asks as the priest meets us at the door. 'About Toto?'

'Isn't he one of the family?' Father Lynch says, kindly. 'Why wouldn't he be welcome in the house of God?'

So we go in, all of us. The organist is playing a slow, sad song that makes me want to slit my wrists, and the church is full of people – old friends, neighbours, distant relatives. They sit in rows, huddled in black coats, navy jackets, silent, respectful.

The coffin is already here, heaped with flowers,

and we have to walk past it to get to the front-row pew that has been set aside for us. I can feel Grandad falter as we file past, but he puts a fist to his mouth and carries on.

Nuala and her family are halfway along the aisle, to the right, and Miss Devlin and Mr McGrath, side by side, and Sue from the hairdresser's. Kristina Kowalski has come too, with Alex. I see them on the other side, two tawny-haired figures, one dressed in a black minidress, the other in a cartoon-knitted sweater and pyjama trousers.

Next to the aisle, down near the front, there's a lanky, straw-haired boy with no shoes, a pair of battered Rollerblades leaning against the kneeler. He grabs my hand as I go past, squeezing it tightly.

We file into the front pew, sit down, Mum and Giovanni, Dad and Victoria, Grandad, Toto and me. We are a family, an unruly, awkward, embarrassing family, but a family all the same. How did I ever think otherwise?

Gran is missing, of course. She was the heart of our mismatched family, but she will never be here again.

The funeral Mass begins. The priest says sad things, lovely things, about Gran, and everyone sings sad hymns and there's a lot of crying, not just in the front pew, and that's OK. Then it's over, and the pall-bearers carry the coffin outside to the big black car that will carry it to the graveyard.

Everyone swarms out of the church then, and that's the hardest bit, because people are hugging me, holding me, pressing my hand, telling me that my gran was a good woman, a wonderful woman, a saint.

'Why didn't you tell me?' Nuala asks when it's her turn. 'About your mum and everything?' I just shake my head, because the reasons seem so small and stupid now.

'I would have understood,' she tells me. 'You know that, don't you, Jude? That's what friends are for.'

'I know,' I say. 'I'm sorry.'

'Idiot,' Nuala says softly. Then, 'I'm sorry about your gran. She was lovely. Remember when she showed us how to make jam tarts, when we were little, and we ate all the jam before the pastry cases were even cooked? She didn't get mad or anything – just sent us down to the corner shop to buy more!'

'She was lovely,' I say, and the word *was* sticks in my throat, like a sliver of glass. Will I ever get used to it?

Nuala moves aside and Kevin Carter walks right up and hugs me tightly, which isn't as scary as you'd imagine. It feels safe and warm and good. 'Thanks, Carter,' I whisper into his neck. 'For everything.'

'S'OK,' Carter says. 'Any time.'

We disentangle, still holding hands. 'So . . .' he says. 'Does this mean you'll go out with me now?'

'Carter!' I kick him on the ankle, and he yelps and backs off and sits down on the church steps, strapping on his Rollerblades. Then Kristina and Alex are in front of me, Kristina's eye make-up all smudged and blotchy with tears.

Nuala, still hovering at my side, does a double take.

'Take care, Jude, OK?' Kristina says, wrapping me briefly in a quick, strawberry-scented hug.

'Take care, Kristina,' I echo, and watch Nuala's jaw drop.

Carter appears on my other side, tottering on Rollerblades. He nods towards Alex. 'Hello,' he says. 'And you are . . . ?'

Alex just squints at him, blankly, and in that moment I can see Carter catching on, working it out, sussing that Alex is different. His face softens.

Kristina catches my eye, biting her lip. I can see the excuses running through her head, ready to drip off her tongue.

'He's my brother,' she says at last, looking from Carter to Nuala, then back again to Alex. 'He's called Alex. OK?'

'Oh! OK,' says Carter, gently. 'Good to meet you, Alex.'

Then suddenly there's a fluttering, a flash of green, and Alex points to the big black hearse, eyes shining. 'Bird!' he says.

There on the big shiny hearse bonnet is a greenfinch, small, vivid, perfect, fluffing up its feathers in the sunshine.

It's October now, and spring is long gone. Summer's over too, and the leaves on the trees that edge the graveyard are turning slowly to scarlet, bronze and gold. There's a chill in the air, and I wind my black scarf tightly around my neck, letting the ends dangle. It's the last scarf Gran ever knitted, and I love it, even though it's full of holes and knots and made from three different kinds of wool.

'What about me?' Carter asks, tugging at the scarf. 'Can't we share?'

We're sitting side by side on the wall that runs alongside the graveyard, looking out at the new-mown grass, the rows of gravestones with their little metal pots filled with supermarket flowers. Carter unpeels the scarf, edges closer to me and wraps it around us both. The fringed ends hang down almost to the ground.

Toto is scrabbling about in the grass at our feet, checking out Carter's abandoned BMX bike, sniffing at the wire-mesh bins filled with rotting flowers, crumpled cellophane. Nearby, the standpipe tap still drips from where I changed the flowers on Gran's grave, rinsed out the metal vase and refilled it.

'I still miss her,' I tell Carter. 'All the time.'

'I suppose you do,' he says.

He doesn't say that I'll get over it, or that the pain will fade with time, like other people do. He just listens, and I think he understands.

'Grandad still sets a place for her at the table, sometimes,' I say. 'Or makes her a mug of cocoa at night. I don't think he'll ever totally believe that she's gone.'

'Well, you get used to people being around,' Carter points out, grinning, digging me in the ribs.

I smile. 'Yeah. Yeah, you do.'

I passed my piano exam, by the way – I even got my Merit. Mum framed the certificate and hung it on the wall in the living room, above the piano, right next to her framed poster of Judy Garland in *The Wizard of Oz*.

Things are different, now, at home. Mum came out of the alcohol dependency unit in May, and right away she signed up for a course the hospital were running on dealing with addiction. She took it seriously, going in every day, learning about alcohol and the way it affects the body. It's a drug, she told me, for some people. She fell in love with drink, loved it more than me or Gran or Grandad, more than Dad or Giovanni. She let it drain the hope out of her life, turn a Technicolor world to black and white.

'Drink wrecks lives,' she said to me. 'You wouldn't believe the damage, the pain it can cause.'

Well, I would, as it goes.

'The trouble is, people don't understand alcoholics,' Mum went on. 'They don't want to be shouted at, or pitied or despised. None of that helps. They need to talk, they need to be understood. And who better to do that than an ex-drinker?'

So now my mum is training to be a voluntary addiction counsellor, which sounds kind of crazy, but then again, in another way, it makes a lot of sense.

Mum called Miss Devlin a few weeks ago, asking about the drama group, and after long discussions, the two of them agreed to organize a production of *The Wizard of Oz* at St Joe's. 'It's a wonderful musical,' Mum insisted. 'With a timeless message. We've all wasted time looking for someone else to fix up all our troubles, haven't we? But nobody else can do that – only we can. We're the ones with the magic.'

'Maybe,' Miss Devlin said. 'I suppose we're all looking for our very own yellow-brick road.'

It's just a matter of time before Miss Devlin

discovers that Mum will be more help with the hair, make-up and costumes than anything else, but hey – that's showbiz.

Giovanni, The One With No Backbone, is still around. His support and encouragement helped Mum get through, and it helped Grandad and me as well. Last month, he sold his ice-cream van on eBay. He hyped it up as a 1960s classic van, and scooped a fortune from some collector down south who reckons he's going to do it up and put it in a museum.

It turns out he's been saving up for years anyway, and he's just put down a deposit on a tiny stall in the food court at the big shopping mall in town. It's going to sell ice-cream sundaes, low-fat sorbets, frozen yoghurts and fresh fruit smoothies, just like Mum suggested. Giovanni will work there full-time, Mum and Grandad part-time, me on Saturdays. Scary.

'At least I don't have to wear a minidress and winkle-pickers,' I tell Carter.

'Shame,' he says, his arm snaking around my waist. 'That dress was cute! I liked the fringy bits.'

I frown. 'How do you know it was cute?' I ask. 'How do you know about the fringy bits?'

Carter looks shifty. 'Your grandad showed me the photos. Last week, when he was helping me fix the buckled wheel on my BMX.'

Carter has abandoned his Rollerblades at last. Brendan Coyle chucked him out of the street hockey team, so he took my advice and found a new hobby. Sadly, his talents – if he has any – do not seem to lie in the world of BMXing, either.

Carter pulls on the long black scarf, reeling me in like a fish on a line until our cheeks are touching. He puts a hand up to push my hair back, tilt my face towards him. He kisses me then, and my lips tingle and my toes curl, and I have to admit that Carter does have talents after all.

After a while, Toto starts whining for attention, and we pull apart, grinning. Carter picks up a fallen branch and chucks it along the cobbled pathway for Toto to chase. It's dusk, and the sky is streaked with pink and orange, casting a golden glow over everything.

'Can't wait to see the next lot of photos,' he says slyly. 'You know, the ones from Italy.'

'You will not be seeing any photos from Italy!' I tell him, sternly.

'What was it you said?' he teases. 'Three metres of apricot-coloured net? Frills and flounces and satin ribbon! A proper bridesmaid's dress, this time. Nice!'

So I elbow him in the side and he yells and wriggles out of the scarf and falls back off the wall into the fallen leaves, waving his legs in the air.

There's going to be another wedding – Mum and Giovanni, this time. They're flying out to Cosenza in Italy, where Giovanni is from, so that his mum, dad, three brothers, four sisters and twenty-two cousins can all be there, along with assorted aunts, uncles and friends.

Grandad and I are going too, of course. It's going to be a church wedding, and Grandad is going to walk down the aisle and give Mum away in time-honoured tradition. Me, I'll be trussed up like an ice-cream sundae, leading six small Italian bridesmaids behind me.

Yippee. I can't wait.

Carter jumps up and sits astride the wall.

'Hey, Jude,' he says, grinning at me. 'How long have we been going out now?'

'We're not going out,' I tell him.

'Right.' He frowns. 'So . . . what are we doing exactly?'

'Just hanging out.'

'Hanging out. OK.' He's so near I can feel his breath, warm and sweet on my cheek. His fingers close around mine.

'Whatever,' he says. 'We've been *hanging out* all summer, yeah?'

'Suppose,' I shrug.

'Well, remember you once said you had to practise something lots to get really good at it?'

'Mmm?'

'I've been thinking about it,' he says, 'and I reckon there are whole aspects of hanging out we haven't even covered yet. It might take months and months – years even – to get it perfect.'

'So?'

'So maybe we should put some more practice in, later. Meet you at the chippy at half seven?'

Carter leans forward and kisses me softly, then jumps off the wall, picks up his BMX and pedals away. Toto runs along behind, nipping at his tyres.

'Watch this!' he shouts, rolling into a wheelie and trying to swat Toto away at the same time. Predictably, the BMX skids off the path and crashes into a wire-mesh bin. Carter sits up, rubbing his elbow.

'I'm getting better!' he says, grinning.

In the setting sun, the cobbled path that cuts through the grass gleams golden yellow. It shimmers in the fading light like something magical, a path that could lead you to an emerald city, glinting in the distance, or maybe just to a night at the chippy with a cute, clumsy, straw-haired boy.

The way I see it, you just have to take your Technicolor moments where you can, before the world fades back into black and white. I slide off the wall and run along the golden path towards Carter, my scarf flying out behind me.

BEST FRIENDS are there for you in the good times and the bad. They can keep a secret and understand the healing power of chocolate.

BEST FRIENDS make you laugh and make you happy. They are there when things go wrong, and never expect any thanks.

BEST FRIENDS are forever,
BEST FRIENDS ROCK!

cathy cassidy's
My
Best Friend
Rocks!
enter at
cathycassidy.com
mizz
award

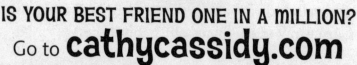

IS YOUR BEST FRIEND ONE IN A MILLION?
Go to **cathycassidy.com**
to find out how you can show your
best friend how much you care